DOGTOWN

A WILLIE BLACK MYSTERY SERIES

DOGTOWN

HOWARD OWEN

THE PERMANENT PRESS
Sag Harbor, NY 11963

For information, address:
   The Permanent Press
   4170 Noyac Road
   Sag Harbor, NY 11963
   www.thepermanentpress.com

Library of Congress Cataloging-in-Publication Data

   Owen, Howard, author.
      Dogtown / Howard Owen.
      The Permanent Press (Sag Harbor, New York), other.
      Sag Harbor, NY: The Permanent Press, 2022.
      Series: A Willie Black Mystery Series
      ISBN 978-1-57962-665-5 (cloth
      ISBN 978-1-57962-666-2 (paper)

   PS3565.W552 D64 2022
   813'.54—dc23/eng/20221205   2022057699

To Karen, as always

CHAPTER ONE

Tuesday, January 5, 2021

SOME KIDS, playing where they shouldn't have been, found it.

They said they saw a hand sticking up out of the weeds. When they got brave enough to go closer, they found the body.

It was just down the hill from a microbrewery that affords a passable ale and a nice view of Richmond's skyline. Of course, nobody much is admiring the skyline from a Dogtown beer hall these days. Bars are temporary victims of the goddamn plague that our former president told us would "just go away" when it got warm last summer. It got warm. It got cold. We're still waiting.

Had he not been dead, the poor sap the kids found might have been entranced by the city's downtown lights, still done up for Christmas, twinkling across the James. Since his throat was cut from ear to ear, however, it is likely that the panorama went unappreciated.

Our chief, L.D. Jones, is on the scene when I get there at three in the afternoon. The site is maybe two minutes off the south side of the Manchester Bridge. I park two blocks away on West Sixth and manage to arrive while the cops are still in the process of figuring out what the fuck happened.

I'm able to talk to one of the still-spooked kids.

"We didn't do nothin'," the boy said, no doubt used to people assuming the worst. The investigating officers probably have already scared the shit out of him.

Even if he didn't gill himself, the guy will not be our first homicide of the year. Nah, you've got to start way before January 5 for that honor. This year, the prize went to the poor woman on the North Side who caught one of the ten million stray bullets New Year's Eve revelers sent into the air at midnight. What comes up, etc. She was standing in her front yard, enjoying cheap champagne, when the errant slug killed her. It wasn't five minutes past midnight, and already Richmond was up and running in the annual homicide derby. They might never know which idiot's bullet killed her.

In some places, they make a big deal over the first baby born in the new year. We put the first homi on the front page, although this one seems strange enough that it might make it too.

The Dogtown victim was, in the chief's terms, exsanguinated. I'm actually surprised that L.D. is sharing this with me, or that he knew what "exsanguinated" means. Maybe he's getting soft in his old age. Since he regained the job he temporarily lost last year amid the ruckus over Richmond's ex-monumenting of Monument Avenue, he does appear to be showing a kinder, gentler side of his personality.

"Kinder" and "gentler" are, of course, relative.

When I ask for some more basic information, like the victim's name, address, etc., the chief replies, "How the fuck should I know? And when I do know, you won't know until I let you know."

Well, I've had a glimpse at the body, and he doesn't fit the profile. Most of our homicide victims here in the Holy City tend to be young and Black. This one looks like he's maybe in his late fifties, and he's Caucasian. Maybe, I'm thinking, drug deal gone bad. Maybe he wandered out of his comfort zone to feed his habit and picked the wrong corner on the wrong night.

But he doesn't look like the type, even in his present diminished state. His clothes aren't fancy, but they're nice enough, the kind worn by a working man trying to make a good impression on the clients.

They put him in the bag and zip it up. Off to the morgue. The crime scene is marked off so that Richmond's finest can wade through the underbrush looking for clues.

I spy Chauncey Gillespie, my favorite donut-devouring flatfoot, slouching against his car, talking to a couple of other cops.

When the other two move away, I go over and ask Gillespie if there's anything he can tell me, anything I don't know already.

He looks around, making sure the chief isn't looking in his direction. Talking to me, in L.D.'s book, constitutes consorting with the enemy.

"Somebody didn't like the son of a bitch," he mutters. "They damn near cut his head off."

"I saw that," I tell him, "but was there anything, like, weird? I mean, weirder than that? Anything you don't normally see in the recently deceased?"

Gillespie suddenly sits up straight and moves away from me like I've tested positive. I look around and see the chief looking our way. He's scowling more than usual. If L.D. ever figured out that I get my inside information from his very own media relations person, the inestimable Pechera "Peachy" Love, he might not give Gillespie such a hard time for occasionally talking to me.

I stand outside the yellow crime tape and look out across the river, where herons are fishing, and a falcon dive-bombs from his aerie atop one of our semi-high-rises.

When I get back to the office, I'll call Peachy and try to put enough pieces together to file something for tomorrow's paper and, of course, our website.

✦ ✦ ✦

THE NEWSROOM is quiet, its default mode these days. Short of selling the office furniture out from under us, the Grimm Group has laid us bare. We have one-third of the news staff we had in our golden days that we didn't know were golden until they turned to shit. No bureaus, no features department, no raises, no bonuses, plenty of layoffs. The last cuts, last summer, took care of the copy desk. We send out for word editing now, same way you do for pizza and Buffalo wings. Some people somewhere in the Midwest that we'll never see and couldn't find Richmond without Google Maps are taking care of that now. From the shape of some of the shit that appears in print under staff bylines, we suspect that the only barrier between raw copy and tomorrow's paper is spell-check.

Sally Velez, my immediate editor and long-ago dating interest, looks up when I come in and asks me where the fuck I've been.

I remind her that it was she who called me at home, as I was getting ready to come in for my night-cops beat, and told me about the dead body in Dogtown.

"Oh, yeah. Shit. Sorry," she says. "I forgot. I've got so many balls in the goddamn air . . ."

"What?"

She says it again. I tell her not to worry about it. Sally's doing the work of about three editors these days, since the other two have been laid off.

Neither of us can hear the other very well, thanks to the COVID masks. If we have to wear these things for five years, I'll still forget to put mine on half the time. Today

I got to the front door of the building where we toil and remembered that I was feloniously breathing fresh air instead of inhaling oxygen tainted by my tuna-salad lunch, so I had to walk back to the car and get the mask.

I fill Sally in on what I saw and heard and promise to have something for the website in fifteen minutes, then something more substantive for our loyal print subscribers who haven't died yet.

The evening goes smoothly enough. On a cold Tuesday night in January, you don't expect a hell of a lot of mayhem on the police beat. Shots were fired in Gilpin Court, but nobody was hit. I do a short on the idiot who tried to rob a convenience store just inside the city limits on the Midlothian Turnpike Monday night, then got caught trying to hit the same place this afternoon. Creature of habit. Otherwise, a good night to play solitaire on the computer.

But then Peachy calls, just after ten.

"I know this won't make the paper," she says, "but you need to know it anyhow." Peachy understands deadlines, because she used to be an honest reporter. I taught her everything I knew in about fifteen minutes. We even saw each other, in the Biblical sense, a few times, when I was between marriages, or almost anyhow. Then, she decided that she'd rather work for the police than the newspaper, which gave the cops a very good media relations person and me a very good clandestine source.

I'm still not free to divulge the victim's name, because the chief hasn't given the OK. Anything to stick it up our butts is the chief's mantra. Peachy gives me the name anyhow, after I promise to sit on it. Otherwise L.D. will know where it came from. Peachy might be out of a job if that happened, and I'd lose my best source.

His name is Harlan Bell. He was a fifty-eight-year-old plumber who lived with his wife over off Semmes Avenue. Peachy says the wife has been contacted, but their son, who lives in Illinois, still hasn't been reached. So nothing for print just yet.

"Any reason why he might have been hanging out down there by the river in Dogtown?"

Peachy says, not for attribution, that it appears he might have been done in elsewhere and then dumped. I'm thinking maybe I can slip that tidbit, from "unnamed source," into the story I've already filed without compromising her.

"No record, as far as we can tell," she says, "other than a couple of speeding tickets."

I hear a commotion in the background.

"Aurora!" Peachy says. "Aurora! Don't put that in your mouth, honey."

A pause and a sigh.

"Well, it's gone now."

Peachy and Ronald are in the process of adopting a little girl whose parents were murdered in our fair city last June, an event that eventually led to my being beaten and kidnapped, although I did get a few good stories out of it.

The couple has also, after "going steady" for some time, gotten married. Aurora would be about fifteen months old now and has gone directly from crawling to running, Peachy says. She also apparently is not a picky eater.

"If it ain't moving," her new mom says, "she's liable to try to swallow it."

I observe that it's nice to see that she isn't overly neurotic about Aurora's dietary habits.

"Aw, hell," Peachy says, "I was the oldest of six, the little momma. I've seen some shit."

She does step away for a few seconds to ensure that her new charge doesn't need the Heimlich maneuver or a trip to the ER. Then she's back.

"Nothing else you can tell me about Mr. Bell?" I ask before we disconnect.

"Well," she says after a few seconds, "there is one thing, but this one's definitely not for attribution until we at least contact all the family, and maybe not then."

The "one thing" was kind of a doozy.

"You probably didn't notice," Peachy says, "but his finger was cut off. The guys on the scene didn't notice it at first, but then one of them saw it. It was his pinky, on his right hand."

"And it wasn't some, like, preexisting condition?"

"Nah. The finger had definitely been cut off postmortem. The medical examiner took a look and said it definitely was done after he was killed. No bleeding or anything."

"And it wasn't lying in the grass?"

"They looked. The doc said it was a clean cut, not like some dog or something gnawed it off."

I thank Peachy for this curious tidbit and promise I won't write anything about it. L.D. will want that finger to remain a secret, in case some masochistic asshole claims he did it and the cops need proof.

✦ ✦ ✦

I GET back to my digs at the Prestwould before midnight, an unusual occurrence. Hell, the bars are shut down. Might as well drink at home.

Cindy is still awake. She's teaching now, going to the school to teach remotely most days while the kiddies get their knowledge at home via Zoom or whatever.

The cats, Butterball and Rags, seem thrilled to see me. Kidding of course. I only get their grudging attention when I come bearing food. Rags, whom I foolishly saved from a feral existence last summer, just sees me as part of the furniture.

Cindy is concerned about the effect COVID-mandated virtual classrooms are having on the youth of Richmond.

"It's just not the same," she said at breakfast this morning. "I can see it in their eyes. I suspect some of them are playing games or checking their email on their iPhones while they're supposed to be paying attention.

"And I can't work up much enthusiasm for busting their chops. Imagine going through what's probably going to be a year and a half of school with none of the social stuff. No sports, no clubs. No prom. Supposedly no dating, although, having been sixteen once, I have my doubts about that."

I observed that there are acts of intimacy that can be done while wearing a mask. She didn't think it was nearly as funny as I did.

As I'm inhaling a Miller longneck, I tell my beloved about my busy day.

"And whoever did it just dumped his body over there by that brewery? Do they know who it was?"

I tell her while swearing her to secrecy for the time being. I don't mention the missing finger.

"Hell," she says, "I know some Bells. I think they lived on Laurel Street, down near the river. You remember them, don't you?"

I shake my head.

"You said his name was Harlan?"

I confirm the name.

"Let me see something," she says as she gets up, leaving me with the felines for company. I flick a peanut at Butterball, who hisses at me.

Cindy comes back with her high school yearbooks, all four of them. She's sentimental, at least compared to me. I think I left my yearbooks at the apartment when I deserted Jeanette, my first wife, about thirty-five years ago.

"Here it is," she says.

She flips to the seniors' pages from her sophomore year.

There he is. Harlan Bell.

"Could it be the same one?" she asks.

It's possible, I concede, adding that he looked a lot worse this afternoon than he did in his senior-class picture. Lying in a field with your throat cut will do that.

CHAPTER TWO

Thursday, January 7

WHO KILLED Harlan Bell and why remain mysteries.

Mrs. Bell, who was kind enough to let me interview her in her grief, said her late husband "didn't have an enemy in the world." To my knowledge, the cops haven't been able to dig up any either.

He left Oregon Hill after high school to take a job working for an uncle in some town in the Shenandoah Valley. He married a girl from there, and he went to school to become a plumber. From my personal experience, this is a better career move than going to college and majoring in journalism. The last plumbing bill I passed on to Kate, my landlady and third former wife, was well into four figures.

"What the hell, Willie?" she inquired. "Did you and Cindy redo the bathroom?"

The Prestwould's pipes, like the building itself, are reaching their centennial and often show their age. Thank God it wasn't my money.

Harlan Bell and his wife eventually moved back to Richmond more than twenty years ago. They have a couple of grown kids in the area. L.D. Jones told me, off the record, that the neighbors all thought he was great, that he'd do little plumbing jobs for them for free. He was an elder in his Baptist church.

Doris Bell said her husband went out on a job somewhere in the West End and never returned.

She reported him missing that night, about eighteen hours before those kids found his body.

Yesterday they found his truck parked at the end of a dead-end dirt road a few miles west of the house where he was supposed to be working. There was a considerable amount of blood in it. The people who hired him said he never showed up for work on Tuesday.

When reportedly good people get murdered by parties unknown for no apparent reason, it raises more concern than your average killing. Yesterday a man was shot and killed sitting in his car over in the East End, but Peachy told me that the guy was in the most lucrative occupation to which a young man from the poor side of town can aspire, and that the suspected shooter was a rival dealer. There was, in other words, some logic in finding him bleeding out in his fine Chevy Tahoe.

There is no apparent logic to Harlan Bell's murder.

"Plus," said Marshall Pitts, our fine publication's first Black columnist, "he was white."

Well, yeah, there was that. I want to believe the murder of an upstanding, God-fearing African American would have gotten the same amount of attention from our readers. I want to believe. As a man with a Black father and white mother, I do feel qualified to see both sides.

I mentioned this to Marshall, who said that being raised in Crackerville by a white woman, I was hardly qualified to weigh in on the issue.

This led me to suggest that Marshall go fuck himself. He chose to take exception to my words, which led to the closest thing the paper has seen to a fistfight in the newsroom in some time. Back when drinking on the job was not seen as a firing offense and some staffers were known to

consume vodka from Styrofoam cups while writing deathless prose, there was the occasional dustup.

Marshall and I were in the process of returning to those
thrilling days of yesteryear when Sarah Goodnight came
out of her office and threatened to fire both our asses if
we didn't grow up.

Marshall's over fifty and I'm sixty, so any further "growing up" seems unlikely. It was daunting, though, to have a
thirty-something boss who used to be my protégé publicly
point out my immaturity.

So Marshall and I shook hands. I stopped by his desk
later, and we had a civil chat about our differences. What
Marshall Pitts won't ever understand, having grown up the
son of a judge living out in Henrico County, is what a per-
spective you get on race when you're the only semi-Black
kid within sight in a tough neighborhood where everyone
knows your parents never got married.

The story I wrote for this morning's readers had all
the background on Mr. Bell, along with testimonials from
everyone but his dog. It gave the details on his truck. I
noted that his wallet, minus any charge cards and whatever cash he had, was in his pants pocket when the body
was found.

I asked the chief about the finger. Of course, he wanted
to know how the fuck I knew about the missing digit. I lied
and said I noticed it when I saw the body on Tuesday. He
told me what Peachy did, that that information should not
be divulged yet.

"But your folks didn't find any missing body parts out
there?"

"If they did, I wouldn't tell you," he replied. "We want
to keep that part quiet for now, and I'd appreciate it if you
did the same."

I'd already promised that to Peachy, but now maybe L.D.
figures he owes me a small debt. If he doesn't remember
my kindness, I'll remind him next time I need information.

The stories in the Wednesday paper and this morning's edition got plenty of reader response, most of it disheartening. I try not to go down the rabbit-hole of our subscribers' comments, but sometimes I just can't help myself.

Two respondees managed to blame the deceased. "What was he doing out there, in that part of town?" one asked, somehow missing the part where the body had almost surely been dispatched elsewhere.

Half a dozen immediately drew the conclusion that he obviously was killed by "thugs," the latest code term racists use now that the N-word is not so acceptable.

One genius living in some Podunk town fifty miles away used Mr. Bell's demise as an excuse to bloviate about the ills of living in a "big city like Richmond, with all its big-city problems."

"Like he could find Richmond with a road map," Sally Velez said. "And where does he come off calling us a big city?"

✦ ✦ ✦

TONIGHT IS quiet enough, until it isn't.

A heads-up from Peachy sometime after nine o'clock alerts me that something bad happened over in Westover Hills.

I round up Chip Grooms from photo, and we make the trip through the Fan, past Byrd Park, and over the Nickel Bridge in fifteen minutes flat.

We find the cop caravan over on Prince Edward Road, a couple of blocks west of Westover Hills Boulevard. They've converged on a two-story brick house that probably offers a nice view of the James, down below and a block over, in the daylight. On a cold January night, it isn't all that inviting.

We're still in Dogtown, but more the show-dog part of it rather than the mutt section. The homes seem very pleasant, middle- to upper-middle-class, even if you can hear a freight train down below from where I'm parked, slogging along at the river's edge, hauling coal to Hampton Roads.

Grooms, who didn't grow up here, asks me why everything in the city south of the river is called Dogtown.

I explain, while looking for somebody in uniform who might talk to me, that the part of the area where the river curves around from north-south to east-west, up around where Harlan Bell's body was found Tuesday, kind of resembles a dog's head, if you squinted your eyes and used your imagination.

As opposed to our condo unit, which seems to be turning into Cat Town.

No, Grooms assures me. He does not want a cat.

I find Gillespie and a couple of his buddies leaning against one of the cop cars, trying not to freeze. Drinking coffee, like so many things, is not so easy when you're wearing a COVID mask, so our men in blue have dispensed with them momentarily. Finding a chance to sneak a Camel, I do the same.

None of them seem surprised, or delighted, to see me there.

"We ain't got nothin' to say to you," the youngest one tells me before walking off. The second one soon departs too.

Gillespie steps out of the glow of the streetlights, and I follow him. I tell him what I already know: that there are two dead bodies in that house, unless they've been removed already.

Chauncey Gillespie doesn't really have much reason to give me a break. I got him in a world of trouble more than a decade ago after his ham-handedness led to the death of a deranged neighbor of mine at the Prestwould, but we seem to have more or less forgiven each other for that unfortunate incident. Call it personal growth.

He confirms that the cops did find two dead bodies inside, but he either doesn't know or won't tell me anything else. As we're talking, I see the front door open and then guys come out carrying two bags.

I see a couple standing in the yard next door, on the other side of a hedge that must be the property line.

They appear to be in their seventies or beyond, and they look pretty rattled. I identify myself and ask them if they know anything about what happened.

The husband asks me who I am. I tell him.

"No names," he says. "I don't want anything in the damn paper."

I assure them both that I'm just an honest journalist trying to do my job, and that I don't even need to know their names.

This seems to satisfy them.

"We've known them since they moved in, must have been twenty years ago. No, nineteen. Right after 9-11," the wife says. "That's how I remember."

Their names are Jack and Sheila McCaskill. Hubby says they're "about seventy-five."

"That's right," his wife says. "Remember, we did that seventy-fifth birthday thing for Jack last fall. We couldn't do much, with the pandemic and all, but we all gathered outside, right here on the front lawn, and did the best we could. We had a cake."

She's tearing up.

"They were perfect neighbors," Hubby says. "Never harmed a soul."

He says one of their other neighbors found their bodies.

"Bob, who lives on the other side of the McCaskills from us, went over for something or other, and he saw the front door was cracked open. He went inside, and, well, he found them.

"He called 911, I guess. When they got here, he was outside and told us what happened."

As delicately as I can, I ask them for any details that Bob, who seems to have left the scene, might have given them about what he witnessed.

The husband shakes his head.

"He just said it was the worst thing he'd ever seen. There was blood every damn where. He said it looked like they'd been tied up and just butchered."

They confirm that no one else was residing in the house.

"They have a son who lives somewhere in town and a daughter, living down in North Carolina, Raleigh, I believe. But nobody lived with them, just Jack and Sheila."

I see L.D. and a couple of his officers exiting the house. I catch up with him and ask him if he can tell me anything about the deceased.

He is, as usual, thrilled to see me.

"What the fuck are you doing here?" he asks by way of greeting.

He always asks, and I always have to tell him.

I also tell him that I understand that their names were Jack and Sheila McCaskill.

"You didn't get that from me," he says. "I'm not confirming anything right now. We had to get in touch with the next of kin."

"So they're dead?"

The chief guesses he can tell me that much.

"I hear there was a lot of blood," I remark.

"Dammit, Willie, I'm not telling you anything else until we get the crime scene secured."

And he walks off.

I collect Grooms, who managed to get a couple of shots of those corpse-laden bundles as they were carried out the front door, and we head back to the paper.

I feel comfortable reporting, for our online audience and tomorrow's print edition perusers, that two bodies were found in a home on Prince Edward Road in Westover Hills. I check with Peachy about ten thirty, and she confirms that the McCaskills' grown children have been notified, so I'm comfortable using the victims' names. I've already looked up scant information on Jack and Sheila McCaskill—their ages, the fact that Jack was a retired banker, and Sheila had worked for the state. They moved here from Staunton nineteen years ago, just like their neighbors said.

I ask Peachy if I can bang out something quick for the paper and call her right back.

Peachy's a pro. She left Ronald with the sleeping Aurora and went into police headquarters when she heard about the apparent double homi.

"Now," I say to my old friend and source when I call back, "tell me what you can tell me, not for attribution."

"Nah," Peachy says. "It's got to be off the record. You want to go with it, you've got to confirm it somewhere else."

I agree. Peachy can tell me what she knows, but I've got to make it for-print official elsewhere. She doesn't want the chief wondering who the "informed source" is.

"He's starting to act kind of funny," she says, "like maybe he knows I've talked to you."

Especially, I'm thinking, since tomorrow's story will have her confirming the McCaskills' identity.

"The neighbors told me there was a lot of blood," I say, to get the conversation going.

"Yeah, you could say that. Again, this is off the record, but there were some similarities to that thing over by the brewery on Tuesday."

"Like what?"

A pause.

"Like both their throats were cut."

OK, Peachy really has my attention now.

"You mean, like the Bell guy?"

"Pretty much so, yeah."

I figure I can find the man who lived next door, Bob, and get him to confirm about the throats, assuming he got a good look at their bodies. Can't do that tonight, but tomorrow I'll be paying a visit.

"Anything else?"

Peachy is quiet for a few seconds.

"OK," she says at last, "I'm going to tell you this, but it really, really can't ever come back to me."

I make myself wait for it.

"The fingers," she says. "Whoever it was, he cut off two of the husband's fingers. One of the cops told me about it."

"Which two?"

"Um, he said the pinky and ring fingers on the right hand."

I promise Peachy that nothing about the missing digits will ever be traced back to her.

Sarah is still in her office. She and I are the last ones to leave our desiccated newsroom tonight. The Grimm Group has shrunk us to the point that advertising and news share the same big space. Where our proud operation used to take up three full floors, most of us fit on one now. This is a good thing, since Grimm sold the goddamn building a couple of years ago. Our landlord rents us the second floor. Even Benson Stine, our esteemed publisher, now has to work on the same floor with the *hoi polloi*.

Sarah's just logging off in expectation of getting home to her husband before midnight when I tell her we might have a bigger story than we expected.

She sits back down.

"Holy shit," she says.

Holy shit indeed. When word gets out that three seemingly decent, middle-class white folks had their throats cut maybe a mile and a half from each other, two days apart, the populace will go nuts.

Sarah knew about the Bell guy's finger, and why we can't print that detail just yet. When I tell her that the guy, assuming it's a guy and the same guy, has upped his game, finger-wise, I can see that her horror is tempered with the kind of excitement that gives hopeless news addicts our fix. Yeah, we feel bad for the victims, really bad, but if you gave us truth serum, I'd have to admit that a story like this gives me a hard-on. I'm pretty sure Sarah is feeling a little damp.

"But if the guy did it again, same method, same thing with the finger or fingers, we need to let people know."

"Be a good time to invest in some firearms stock," I observe.

"Yeah, folks will go crazy, but we still have a civic duty to let people know there's a maniac on the loose."

That's true. Somebody, and I guess it's me, has to have a heart-to-heart with L.D. about putting Richmond on alert that there's a serious nutjob out there.

I tell Sarah that I'll get in touch with this Bob character tomorrow, and if he can confirm the thing about the fingers, I'll pay the chief an unwelcome visit.

✦ ✦ ✦

I GET home before midnight. My old friend and our apartment mate Abe Custalow is already in bed, but Cindy has waited up for me. Butterball and Rags have sidled up to her on the couch, silently daring me to intrude on their space.

My beloved bitches a little about the lunacy of trying to teach high school kids via Zoom, and how the ones she really feels sorry for are the teachers and kids in the lower grades.

I let her vent while I go to the fridge for a beer.

"So," she says when I come back into the living room, "how was your night?"

CHAPTER THREE

Friday, January 8

BOB'S NAME—honest to God—is Bob White. A question I'd like to ask him: Couldn't you have called yourself Bobby or Rob or Robbie or Robert or anything that didn't make your name sound like a damn quail?

I keep that thought locked in my brain when I go back to Prince Edward Road.

Mr. White cracks his door open with the chain still on it.

"You're not one of those TV people are you?" he asks through the crack.

I assure him that I am not but feel obliged to admit that I do work for the newspaper.

Surprisingly he undoes the latch.

He and I are both wearing masks, so it's kind of hard to tell, but Bob White appears to be a little older than I am. He says he's a longtime subscriber. He even recognizes my name.

"What the hell have you all done with Mark Trail?" he asks, and then launches into a diatribe about the artistic ability and general mental acuity of whoever is doing the comic strip these days. It won't help me get into his good graces if I tell him that I and most of the news staff would have sent Mark and his outdoorsy cohorts to the comics graveyard years ago if it weren't for people like him who raise holy hell every time we try.

Instead I nod sympathetically and promise to personally relay his concerns to our publisher.

"Those TV people are like vultures," Bob says, explaining his earlier trepidation. "I guess they found out I was the one discovered the bodies."

"I did have a couple of questions to ask you about that," I tell him, "but I won't put your name in the paper unless you say it's OK. I just need some information."

He's wearing a sports jacket and a tie, so I assume he's got other things to do today than talk to a nosy-ass reporter. Turns out he's a real-estate agent, and he has to see a couple about a house in less than an hour. He volunteers that having a name like "Bob White" makes it easy for people to remember him. No doubt, I'm thinking.

"This won't take long," I assure him.

I ask about the bodies.

He moves into the living room, and we both sit. He allows that we can take off our masks as long as we don't get too close to each other.

"I've never seen anything like it," he says. "When I opened the door, Sheila was lying there, maybe five feet from the door, like she was trying to get away. I followed the blood and found Bob in the kitchen. There was so much blood. When I got home later, it was all on the soles of my shoes. I've thrown 'em away."

He confirms the fact that their throats had been cut.

"There might have been other cuts, but that was what you noticed. They were just slaughtered."

He looks a little pale and takes a few deep breaths before he goes on.

"They were the nicest folks you'd ever want for neighbors," he says when he continues. "Never had a cross word with them."

I get to the crux of my inquiry.

"Mr. White, was there anything you noticed about Mr. McCaskill's hands?"

He looks up.

"Like what?"

"Was there any damage to his hands that you could see?"

He thinks on it for a few seconds.

"There was so much blood everywhere, it was hard to tell but, yeah, his hand was kind of a mess, like he'd been stuck pretty good there too."

"Do you remember which hand?"

He visualizes it in his mind.

"I think right. Yes, it definitely was his right hand."

He asks the obvious question.

"Why do you want to know about that?"

There isn't much to do at this point except try to entice Mr. White into being my accomplice.

"Mr. White . . ." I begin.

"Call me Bob," he says.

"Bob," I start over, "I'm a reporter with a problem. A very reliable source has told me that whoever did this apparently cut off two of Jack McCaskill's fingers, on his right hand. I can't go with that information, can't print it, until it's confirmed by somebody else, somebody who saw it."

I explain, as gently as I can, that the police don't like to release this kind of information, but that it is, in my opinion, essential that they do.

"Why?"

I plunge in.

"Because, if what I told you about the fingers is true, then it seems to tie this to another murder earlier this week."

"That guy over by the river?"

I nod my head.

"There might be a serial killer loose out there?"

It's too soon to say, I reply, but it's not looking good.

"So," I tell him, "here's what I need you to do."

I explain that I intend to visit the chief of police and tell him that I have a witness who will confirm that two of Jack McCaskill's fingers had been cut off.

"What I need from you," I tell Bob, "is to tell the chief, his name is L.D. Jones, that you saw that those fingers were cut off. He might not even call, might just take my word for it that you confirmed it to me. Hell, he knows it's true. He just needs to know that I know. And he won't release your name."

"I talked to some detective last night," Bob says, "and I didn't mention anything about his hand."

"Just tell him, if the chief or anybody else asks you, that you forgot, with everything else that you saw."

"So, if anybody asks me, you want me to say I saw Jack's fingers were missing."

He's quiet for a moment.

"Yeah," he says at last, "I can do that. Seems like people should know."

I thank him for his cooperation.

As he's walking me to the door, a safe six feet behind me, he says, "Which fingers?"

Good question. He kind of needs to know that. I tell him: pinky and ring.

Bob nods his head.

"Yeah," he says. "Now that you mention it, I think I did see that. Don't worry, Willie. I've got it."

We bump elbows and he closes the door.

✦ ✦ ✦

"He didn't say a goddamn word about any fuckin' fingers last night!"

The chief is a little perturbed, as he often is when the cone of silence under which he tries to keep all police knowledge is breached.

"But you know it's true, don't you?" I press him. "You must have known. You saw the bodies."

"I didn't see shit," he says. "All I know is what they told me when I got there. And the detective didn't say anything about any fingers."

I don't believe for a minute that L.D. doesn't know. If Peachy knew, L.D. knew. He had to have seen it.

He finally is convinced that Mr. Bob White told me the corpse was missing two fingers, and which ones they were.

He reminds me that I promised not to write about the missing finger on the guy who turned up on Tuesday.

I tell him what he damn well knows already: One stiff with a missing pinky is just kind of weird. Worth keeping quiet about in case somebody confesses and they want details. But two dead guys slightly more than two days apart with missing digits starts to look like a trend.

"People need to know," I say.

"They're just going to go nuts," the chief says.

They're going to go nuttier, I reply, if they find out that their chief of police has been withholding evidence of a serial killer loose in Richmond.

"Better," I advise, "if you tell them yourself."

It's almost noon when we come to an agreement. L.D. will call a press conference for two o'clock, but I'll put the information about the fingers, all three of them, on our website an hour beforehand.

It would warm the cockles of my newspaper heart to have everyone first learn about the fingers in tomorrow's paper, rather than breaking it online and having TV jump all over it on the evening news. Sometimes, though, you have to put the public good first. Even journalists occasionally do that.

Plus, the local video folks will be kind of honor-bound, if they have any, to concede that we broke the story.

✦ ✦ ✦

I'VE FILED on the website by one, leading with the obvious similarities in the homicides. I leave Bob White's name out of it, just write that the information came from the usual "reliable source." I doubt that L.D. will be checking back with White either.

I tell Mal Wheelwright and Sarah Goodnight, my ultimate newsroom bosses, that there will be a press conference in one hour with the chief confirming what we're telling our readers.

Sarah presses me to reveal my source. I have no problem with that, and explain that the guy's a little uneasy, all things considered, about having his name in print. Serial killers read newspapers too.

"Really?" Sarah says. "His name is Bob White?"

"He says it's good for sales."

"Great job," Wheelie says. He adds that he needs to talk to somebody in advertising, because he's pretty sure the local gun purveyors are going to want to take out ads in tomorrow's paper.

I hope he's kidding.

✦ ✦ ✦

THE STORY in this morning's paper only gave readers a bare-bones account of what happened in Westover Hills. Even that, though, was enough to sow a bit of paranoia among them.

There were fifty-eight comments last time I checked, although half of those were two jerks yakking back and forth at each other.

One of them thought the paper was being racist, running a white double homi on A1 "when you got Black folks every day dying back there inside on the same page with those 'Have sex again' ads."

The other one took the tack that most of the Black killings were drug-related and thus not worthy of the front page.

This, not surprisingly, set off a firestorm, with others weighing in between the missiles the two original antagonists fired at each other.

"Why do we even encourage comments?" I asked Wheelie once. "We're like a moron magnet."

"We want it to be a two-way street," was his reply. "We don't want them to think we're just talking at them."

Maybe I'm just a little prickly, two days after a bunch of yahoos, fired up by a sore loser, tried to storm the US Capitol and have a lynch party, but I'm a little ambivalent about freedom of speech today.

For tomorrow's edition, now that we know evil is among us, we're going pedal to the metal on mayhem.

Leighton Byrd has been assigned a story on Richmond's more spectacular serial killings and other mass slaughters over the years. This seems like miscasting to me, since Leighton's only been out of college a little more than two years. However we're a little short on institutional memory around here, having laid off just about anybody who can remember beyond the turn of the century.

"It's not ageism," Ray Long said his lawyer told him when he inquired about legal recourse when he and the rest of the copy desk got laid off. "It's wage-ism."

Yeah, what a coincidence. The older reporters and editors are the ones making the most money.

At any rate, the lovely Leighton seeks my assistance.

"I mean, you've been around, like, forever," she delicately puts it.

I offer to give her my take on the fall of Richmond in 1865.

"You know what I mean. I just need to know some dates for some of the more spectacular murders."

So I give her a quick trip down a blood-spattered memory lane. The Brileys. The Beltway snipers. The Southside Strangler. I suggest the last one might be of particular interest, since it was another bad moment for Dogtown. I mention a couple of more recent ones in which my journalistic input was part of the story.

"Wow," she says when I've ticked off what I consider the low points in Richmond civility, "there's been a lot of bad shit going on around here."

"Well," I reply, "we don't concentrate much on the good news. Nobody wants to read about '28 days since the last murder.' We're no better or worse than anywhere else. I hope."

Leighton's a good reporter. She reminds me a little of Sarah, whom I helped wean in her early days here and with whom I committed misdemeanor hanky-panky, a fact about which we have mutual, willful amnesia now that she's my boss. Leighton's a little hard-nosed, some might say hard-hearted, but the sweet-natured ones don't seem to stick around that long.

When Leighton later shows me what she's written, I don't really have many quibbles. Considering that this is ancient history to her, she did a pretty good job, and I tell her so.

"When are you going to buy me a beer?" she asks.

When we can sit at a bar again, I tell her. When this damn COVID shit is past.

"Well, I'm waiting," she says and gives me a wicked little grin. "Any time."

In the old days, when I was in the disposable marriage business, Leighton and I might have enjoyed some off-the-clock mischief, but I'm getting to that harmless age, where you figure that if anyone as attractive and young as Leighton would be willing to share the sheets, it would be a mercy fuck.

Plus I really, really want Marriage No. 4 to work. Cindy knows enough of my checkered past to suspect the worst, even at my advanced age.

✦ ✦ ✦

FOR TOMORROW'S paper, I expand on what I put in the e-paper, getting as much information as I can about the deceased and describing, in inevitably gory detail, how they died. The one guy responsible for graphics puts together a map showing the proximity of the slayings to each other. I even get up with some folks in Oregon Hill who knew Harlan Bell since before he left Richmond and then returned. By Hill standards, he was a model citizen. Only got kicked out of school once and eventually graduated.

If the cops have any clue about why Harlan Bell and Jack and Sheila McCaskill were dispatched, they're not talking.

All we can do is further alarm the populace and give gun sales a boost.

✦ ✦ ✦

AND, BECAUSE crime never sleeps, I have to go out to a shooting on the North Side, a couple of blocks east of Chamberlayne Avenue.

The kid who was shot was, I learn, seventeen years old. Of course, nobody saw anything, but I do learn from one of the other kids standing around that "some dudes just come by and started shooting." He didn't know what kind of car, or who was in it. Couldn't even remember what color it was. I asked him about race and he just looked at me like I was dumb as a rock.

As I'm leaving the scene, I hear a voice from the crowd.

"Hey, newspaper man," the voice says, "why don't you put this on the front page?"

Others seem to pick up on his complaint.

OK, he's got a point. Black kid gets gunned down, and we assume it was drug-related and so he somehow had it coming, and we bury it inside somewhere.

But how the hell do you downplay it when three people of any color with no criminal records and seemingly minding their own business, get slaughtered?

The only wise tactic is to put your head down and get the hell out of there.

CHAPTER FOUR

Saturday, January 9

RICHMOND IS in full-blown panic mode.

The TV stations can't stop running pictures of those three older white people who got murdered this week. Our city is about 50 percent Black, but about four-fifths of our murder victims are African Americans. So white homicides are outliers. They sell newspapers and boost TV ratings among our paler patrons.

Callie Ann Boatwright did a story for this morning's readers on the local gun shops, who are having the best week since last November's election last brought out the crazies. And apparently everybody who buys a weapon isn't taking gun-safety classes. One page over from Callie Ann's story was one in which some would-be Wyatt Earp out in Mechanicsville shot himself in the leg while showing family and friends how good he was at twirling his six-shooter.

The lead story, of course, is about the killings themselves. Other than the detached digits, there wasn't much new to write for our Saturday audience, just more BS from the chief about "ongoing investigation" and "following up on several leads." Truth is, according to Peachy, the cops are still flying blind.

The investigators apparently didn't find much in the way of fingerprints or blood at either site that didn't belong to the victims, and the perp apparently was conscientious enough to take his murder weapon, evidently a big-ass knife, with him.

A serial killer was about the only thing that could take everybody's No. 1 concern off the top of the front page: vaccines.

A month ago, it looked like we'd be waiting until late spring to get our anti-COVID silver bullets. Then the vaccine started drifting out to the public, in no discernible pattern, and folks who were resigned to waiting suddenly wanted their fair share right damn now.

A story leaks out that the city or one of the counties is taking reservations for the first of the two shots the experts tell us we need to ward off the plague. Then after half the populace spends an hour or two trying to log on to the appropriate site, we find out that, oops, technical error. No vaccine.

People lucky enough to get a slot sit in their cars idling in tedious lines at the NASCAR track or elsewhere. Even though the first doses are supposed to go to essential workers and people even older than me, there's the usual line-jumping.

What's funny, in a not-so-funny way, is that a large minority of idiots say they won't take the vaccine, while the rest of the population is willing to mug nurses and step over invalids to get it.

People are driving all the way to North Carolina when they learn that some jerkwater town in the middle of a tobacco field somehow has landed a batch of the magic potion. We had one case of a man who desperately needed it driving all the way to Abingdon, which is about as far from Richmond as New York City although the trip is somewhat more scenic.

An armed citizenry desperate for something they think could save their lives can lead to unfortunate consequences. Yesterday shots were fired at the raceway vaccination site when one of the hopeful recipients thought another guy had cut him off as they jockeyed for pole position. Fortunately the guy was a lousy shot and was soon disarmed and pulled from the field by a county deputy.

Sometimes the anti-vaxxers have a change of heart. Jerry Cannady, my mother Peggy's lame-ass neighbor, had been telling her and anyone else who would listen that he wasn't going to take the vaccine, that it was just a Democratic hoax, I guess to turn us all into liberals. And then, two days ago, Peggy said Cannady and his idiot brother had driven to some town up on the Northern Neck because a cousin of theirs said the vaccine was available there.

"Didn't do him no good though," my old mom said, her chortle breaking into a hacker's cough. "When he got there, they weren't giving shots to anybody but people that lived in that county."

Good, malevolent Willie thought. Fuck him. If a Democrat told Cannady the sun rose in the east, he'd call it fake news. Let him fake his ass out of a ventilator.

Peggy and Awesome Dude, her peripatetic perpetual houseguest, have, praise God, gotten their first shots, thanks to the diligence of Andi, my daughter and her granddaughter. Andi, bless her, got up before dawn three days in a row before she glommed on to a site that actually did take reservations and did have the goods. Peggy and Awesome already survived one bout of COVID, last year, but better safe than sorry. And this blows my theory that marijuana can stave off the coronavirus.

Peggy, who has spent much of her adult life moderately stoned, says she's ambivalent about the commonwealth of Virginia's legislature being on the verge of making Satan's weed legal.

"Shoot," she said when I asked her about it, "if they make it legal, it'll take all the fun out of it. And all the amateurs will be toking. It'll be a mess, because they don't know how to handle it."

Maybe, I suggested, she could hold seminars.

✦ ✦ ✦

AT ANY rate, what I'd hoped would be a quiet Saturday got suddenly very loud about the time I normally punch in at the paper.

Sarah called as I was headed to work. Butterball and Rags had watched me go with an impressive lack of interest. I always leave the door open a second or two longer than necessary in the hopes that one or both of the freeloading felines will make a run for freedom and become somebody else's problem. Knowing a meal ticket when they see one, they never take the bait.

"You need to get over to City Hall," Sarah says when I answer my cell out in the hallway. "There's a press conference. They think they've got him."

I park at the paper's lot and walk the six blocks to City Hall, a building whose utilitarian blandness is only accented by the fact that the old City Hall in its fading Gothic granite grandeur is a block over. On the way, I tempt fate and censure by unmasking and smoking a Camel.

The fact that the presser is here instead of at police headquarters tells me that the mayor will be the main act, with L.D. as his warm-up. That's what usually happens when there's good news to impart. Hizzoner, whose long game includes the governor's mansion a few blocks away, is always ready to step in on a moment's notice when the going gets easy.

There's a certain amount of tension between the chief and the mayor these days.

The latter suspended the former last year when Black Lives Matter turned into a free-for-all that left Broad Street with a bunch of boarded-up buildings and the police facing charges of being overenthusiastic in their pursuit of law and order. A cynic would have said the mayor needed a scapegoat. If L.D. hadn't been so good at covering his ass, he'd be enjoying his police pension right now. A certain taped conversation with Hizzoner was enough to convince Our Leader to let the chief keep his job, but it's hard to see the love these days when the two of them share space.

L.D. gets up and tells us the basics: A drifter was arrested earlier outside a convenience store over near VCU. The man was wearing a watch that apparently had previously belonged to one Harlan Bell. It had Bell's initials on it. He also had the late Mr. Bell's VISA card, which he stupidly used at the convenience store on Grace where pretty much everybody deals in cash, one of those places that keeps the bars on the windows 24/7.

"The attendant grew suspicious because he said that the suspect did not appear to be a person who would have a credit card," L.D. says.

Plus, the clerk could read and recognized the name on the card.

The chief passes out copies of the guy's photo and basic information to me, the TV grunts, and the guy from the alternative (read: Black) weekly.

The suspect's name is Sylvester Simms, nickname "Sly." Jesus Christ, the guy looks like one of those unfortunates who stand on the busier street corners here, begging change from motorists.

He appears to be white, although grime and a life on the streets seem to have given him an unhealthy tan, kind of like a piece of leather that's been left out in the sun and rain for a hundred years. His eyes aren't exactly focused, and when he looks like he's trying to smile, his teeth are brown and scarce.

His address, which I could have guessed, is Unknown.

Before I or anyone else can ask the chief any questions, the mayor steps in. He's wearing well-pressed jeans and a button-down shirt, his imitation of a hard-working African American executive taking time off from his busy weekend to calm the masses.

"We are pleased to announce that we have apprehended the man believed to have committed the atrocious crimes that have so alarmed us over the last week," says the mayor. "We want everyone to know that this is not acceptable, that Richmond is a peaceful city where evil will be pulled out by its roots whenever it springs up."

I see L.D. roll his eyes behind Hizzoner and whisper something to his second in command. It is hard to miss the fact that the mayor does his whole self-congratulatory strut without ever mentioning his police force.

After a couple minutes more of blathering about Richmond's greatness and future, the mayor steps back to field questions.

"Chief," I call out. I can see that the mayor is hurt that he isn't seen as the answer man here.

"Willie," L.D. says, in much the same tone as he might have said "COVID."

"This man, Mr. Simms, can you tell us something about how your men apprehended him?"

I'm trying to give the chief a chance to shine, to let the TV folk know who really did the work here.

He explains that the store's manager called the cops as soon as Simms left the store, and that he was "apprehended" outside sitting on the concrete ledge at the edge of the store's tiny parking lot, drinking from a bottle of Tuesday vintage wine.

"And he didn't put up a struggle?"

The chief allows that this was the case.

"He knew that we had him. He still had the deceased's charge card on him."

"And he confessed?"

The chief nods. "He did."

"To all three killings?"

L.D. hesitates. Uh-oh.

"He did," he says finally. "Eventually."

I ask for some more elucidation on what "eventually" means.

"I'm not at liberty," the chief says, "to divulge every single word of the interview, but rest assured that Mr. Simms did confess. To all three murders."

The guy from the weekly has a question.

"The suspect seems to be white," he says. "Can we expect him to get the same kind of justice a Black man would have gotten had he committed such heinous crimes?"

L.D. looks like he's about to explode, but he holds it in and explains, slowly and patiently, to the white reporter for a paper whose audience is Black, why, as a Black police chief, he is not inclined to have a different standard for African Americans.

The reporter smirks, his barb spent.

The TV folk ask the chief a lot of redundant questions, mostly so they can have video on the six o'clock news of their own good-hair selves playing reporter.

I do have time to ask the chief one more question before he takes his leave.

"Do you think that Mr. Simms is competent?"

The chief, who is trying to escape by now, stops.

"What do you mean, competent?"

"Competent. Capable of knowing what he's doing. Sane?"

L.D. is getting a little exasperated and trying not to show it with the cameras rolling.

"He seemed 'competent' enough to me," the chief says, using air quotes. "He was competent enough to steal a watch and credit card off a dead man. You'll have to take that up later with a psychiatrist though. I'm just a dumb ol' police chief."

The mayor, who always enjoys seeing L.D. fighting not to channel his inner Yosemite Sam, thanks the news media for coming.

The chief leaves, throwing me a glance that could only be described as baleful.

✦ ✦ ✦

THE GOOD news that our serial killer has been caught is all the rage on the local TV stations. There isn't much for me to write that our readers won't already know when they get the Sunday paper.

It does occur to me, though, that Sly Simms looks, from the police mug shot, to be one of your more unlikely mass murderers.

For one thing, the guy is listed as five foot four, weighing 120 pounds. Mighty small for a guy who was able to murder three reasonably healthy citizens with a knife.

The fact that he has no fixed address encourages me to check in with the one person I know best whose address often was not fixed before Peggy took him in.

I've known Awesome Dude since I was a young reporter, and he was pretending to be a student at Virginia Commonwealth University. His greeting on any occasion from a party to a funeral was "Awesome, Dude," so we started calling him that. We didn't encourage him to legally change his name, which he did anyhow.

What possessed Awesome's parents to send him to college is beyond me. Maybe blind hope that their strange

kid would suddenly grow brain cells. What possessed VCU
to accept him is an even greater puzzle.

His undergraduate days didn't last long. He hung
around the campus, though, doing odd jobs and living the
student life, without the pesky classes or books. Eventually he became homeless, depending on a stipend his
family sent him, probably to ensure that he didn't come
back, for necessities like food and dope.

He and I have had a symbiotic relationship. Over the
years, I'd slip him a few dollars now and then, and he'd tell
me shit that nobody in the "real" world knew.

Awesome's fifty-five years old, missing a few teeth.
His hair has turned white. I can't imagine that he and my
seventy-eight-year-old mom are sharing a bed, an image
I try to never let invade my cranial cavity. He still tells
me things. He is prone to disappear now and then for a
few days at a time, visiting old friends who still camp by
the river or beneath overpasses and frequent the shelters
when it's too cold to sleep outdoors. I think he's happy to
have a roof over his addled head, but he does sometimes
hear the call of the wild, which means he goes places and
knows things. I figure he might have crossed paths with
Sly Simms.

Bingo.

"Sly Dog?" Awesome asks when Peggy gets him on the
phone. "Yeah, I know Ol' Sly. What you asking about him for?"

It turns out that Peggy and her houseguest haven't
tuned in to the evening news.

I fill him in.

"No, that ain't right! No!" Awesome says. "That can't
be right."

I assure him that it is.

"Can you tell me anything about Sly Simms?"

He tells me that he has known the man in police custody "for maybe fifteen years. Didn't know his last name

until I had to go with him one day to help him straighten out something with his disability check."

Awesome says Simms told him he was hurt in a construction accident.

"A load of bricks fell on him, and he wasn't right after that," he said.

I ask how fit Awesome thinks his old acquaintance is.

"Fit! Hell, Willie, you know how hard it is to get disability in this state? Did you ever see him walk?"

"Haven't seen him at all."

"Well, he looks like he's drunk, even when he ain't. He's kind of wobbly, you know, like he needed to take one of them Deathalyzer tests."

I'm thinking it's going to be hard to get that kind of detail into a story, especially since I haven't seen Simms in the flesh.

"But you say he's harmless."

"Aw, man. I never seen him lay a hand on nobody in anger. He just wanted to be left alone."

I tell Awesome about how they caught him.

"He took a dead man's charge card?" the Dude says.

"Assuming he didn't take the card first and then kill him."

"Well," Awesome says, "I didn't say he was no saint. I mean, the guy wasn't going to be using that charge card anymore, was he? But ain't no way Sly Simms killed anybody. And with a knife? Damn, Willie. I saw him near-bout pass out one day when they was giving him a flu shot at the clinic."

"But he confessed."

"I seen lots of people confess. Guys would tell stories, down by the river, about what the cops would do to them. And a guy like Sly? Man, I bet they could of got him to say anything. He's weak-minded, Willie."

Coming from Awesome Dude, that's quite an indictment.

But I am aware that L.D.'s guys are capable of getting the innocent to confess, given enough time and pressure.

And so, I take a chance and use what my unattributed source has told me to put something together for Sunday's paper, a little more than the video crowd offered up at six and eleven.

I call L.D. at home for a response. He gave me his cell number years ago and occasionally regrets it. He's never that happy to talk to me, and I didn't endear myself to him at the press conference.

Plus it's after eight when I call, and I figure the chief's dipped his beak into the Scotch a time or three since dinner.

"Never call me at home," is his greeting when my number comes up on his phone.

"But you gave me your number, L.D."

"That was emergencies, goddammit."

I explain that this isn't exactly an emergency, more of a courtesy call.

"When did you ever show anybody any courtesy?"

I tell him that there's going to be something in tomorrow's paper about the physical and mental stability of his prisoner.

"You're just stirring up shit," the chief says. I can hear the ice cubes tinkling in the background, along with a Fats Waller tune. "I could see that coming from the shit you were asking at the press conference. The man confessed."

My source, I tell L.D., says the man is damn near crippled, that he can't even walk straight, and that he has the reputation in his community for being mild as a lamb.

"His community!" the chief explodes. "You mean those bums that live down at Texas Beach? That's your source?"

So, I tell him, give me something that refutes what I've been told by my reliable source.

"We caught him with a murdered man's charge card. He confessed to killing not only Bell but also that couple in Westover Hills. What the hell else do you want? Video?"

I ask L.D. if Simms volunteered that he murdered the McCaskills.

"What do you mean, 'volunteered'? He said he did them."

I dig a little deeper.

"Did somebody ask him, before he confessed, if he killed the couple? Did he tell them about the fingers, or did your guys ask him if he cut off their fingers?"

The chief loses any pretense of being patient.

"Goddammit, Willie, he confessed. We didn't have to ask him anything about any fuckin' fingers. Plus he could've read about that in the paper, since you insisted on telling the whole damn world about it."

I thank L.D. for his time. He does not say I'm welcome.

CHAPTER FIVE

Sunday, January 10

CINDY, ABE, and I make the scene at Joe's, reasonably secure that we aren't COVID-infected. R.P. McGonnigal and his latest boyfriend, a lawyer at Dewey, Cheatem and Howe—I might have the firm's name wrong—also are present. And Abe brings along Stella Stellar, whose budding musical career has been somewhat stifled by the fact that live music is deader than eight-track tapes while the pandemic rages.

Cindy's brother, Andy, gave it a pass today, since he apparently came within six feet of somebody who later tested positive.

Cindy says we're not being very safe. I say nothing short of bubble wrap is going to keep us from harm 7/24.

"It stands to reason," she replies, snidely I think, "a man who smokes a pack or two of Camels a day isn't going to be too worried about safety."

The waitstaff has made sure there isn't anyone within ten feet of us at our back table. Hell, they'd probably like to keep us ten feet away from the rest of the customers on a regular basis.

Stella, the former Carla Jean Crump, is bemoaning the fact that she's working the late shift at McDonald's now that her band, the Goldfish Crackers, is gig-less.

"We tried puttin' some shit online, like on YouTube, but it just ain't the same. You don't hear anybody, don't feel the love. Plus we ain't selling hardly any CDs. Our drummer's moved back in with his momma."

Francis Xavier "Goat" Johnson, the Oregon Hill gang's long-distance member, calls from the Ohio college that inexplicably still employs him as its president.

"You all are brave," he says over Zoom. "Hell, we can't even have on-campus classes until probably March."

He appears to be lounging at a cabana on a beach somewhere, but he says that's just a fake background.

"I'm just sitting in my damn study, where I've spent it seems like the last century or so."

We talk a bit about the recent attempted coup at the US Capitol. We agree that the nuts came from all over, although Virginia's proximity to DC sometimes seems to make us an idiot magnet.

"And you've got yourselves a serial killer? Although it looks like they've caught him, if your paper's website isn't full of crap."

Apparently so, I allow.

R.P. picks up on that.

"Apparently? Didn't the asshole confess?"

I ask R.P. if he's aware of how many convicts who confessed have since been exonerated by DNA evidence.

"Aw," his lawyer buddy says, "you're just trying to stir up some crap. Next thing you know, that damn Marcus Green will be representing him."

I don't tell the ambulance-chaser that the next thing on my to-do list after a couple more Bloody Marys and a Nickwich with fries is a call to Richmond's most famous defender of the innocent (and guilty, if the price is right).

"That Pitts guy sure seems to have a burr up his ass," R.P. remarks.

Indeed. Marshall used his Sunday column to rant, as he often does. Today's diatribe was about white privilege, in this case the privilege of having your grisly murders featured on A1 instead of inside among the erectile dysfunction ads.

Nobody wants to admit it, but everybody sees the world through their own filter, and when most of the alleged brain trust at the paper is Caucasian, middle-class white folks getting their throats cut will make the front page. With relatives on both sides of Richmond's most intransigent fence, I've known that for a long time. Is it getting better? Yeah, but not fast enough.

We finish our weekly repast. While Goat is still Zooming with us, we toast Sammy Samms, who would have turned sixty today.

John Wesley Samms was the sixth member of our Oregon Hill rogue's gallery. As kids, he, Goat, R.P., Andy, Abe, and I never really got into serious trouble, not the kind that would earn you a free stay at the state prison down the hill. Sure, Abe did time later, after a stint in the marines, for killing a guy who needed killing, but as teenagers, we weren't guilty of much more than the occasional ass-kicking or penny-ante shoplifting.

We stood out in our little bone-white, redneck world. Custalow, a proud Native American, and I gave the place what color it had. If the general populace at the time had known that R.P. was not romantically inclined toward women, we might have had even more issues with the xenophobic element on the Hill.

Sammy was the only one of us who didn't survive our wild oats days. He wasn't yet thirty when crack cocaine dragged him to an early grave.

"He was the best of all of us," R.P. says, and nobody disagrees.

I propose one more toast, to the absent Andy Peroni, just for being Cindy Peroni Black's brother.

Then, as we're settling up, I get a call.

It's Sarah.

"There's been an incident over in the West End you might want to know about," she says.

She's aware that I have Sundays and Mondays off, so this must be important.

Apparently a twelve-year-old girl was almost abducted right in her neighborhood, a neighborhood where no home sells for much less than seven figures and crime is somebody else's problem.

I am appalled that evil could invade such a privileged enclave, but I wonder out loud why that would cause me to work on Sunday.

"There was a knife," Sarah says.

When I ask her how she knows, she says she can't reveal her source. Either Sarah has her own squealer in blue, or Peachy is cheating on me.

Either way, Sarah has my attention.

✦ ✦ ✦

I DROP Cindy at the Prestwould, promising to be home "soon," and go to the address Sarah gave me.

My destination is a Victorian behemoth set on one of Windsor Farms' more elegant streets, not all that far from the Philadelphia Quarry. It takes me awhile to find the damn thing. The neighborhood must have been laid out by someone with a fondness for mazes.

There are two cop cars parked out front. I see Gillespie leaning on one of them. When I ask him what happened, he's in unhelpful mode and says I'll have to ask the chief.

L.D. comes out a few minutes later. As usual, he has no information to share, beyond the fact that an adolescent was grabbed by an assailant around nine this morning, and that the kid was able to break free.

"And it was a girl?"

"How the fuck . . . ? I'm not at liberty to tell you that."

"But no arrest?"

"It's an ongoing investigation," the chief says. "We expect to have more information soon, and when we do, you'll be notified."

"Was a knife involved?"

L.D. looks up at me in surprise and exasperation.

"We can't say that yet. You're not supposed to know that."

"Thanks for the confirmation."

The chief gets close enough for me to smell his lunch.

"I didn't confirm a damn thing," he says. "And you better not write that I did."

I back off, but L.D. and I both know what this means. How many crazy people can there be running around Richmond terrorizing civilians with knives? Since the cops have one such suspect in custody, today's episode is a little disconcerting.

"Can I talk to the family?" I ask.

"They aren't talking to anybody, and especially not to you," the chief says.

I get the name off the mailbox out front.

Then I drop into the newsroom long enough to look up the residents of the house in Windsor Farms.

I call the one person I know who probably is no more than one degree of separation from anyone in that pricey neighborhood.

Clara Westbrook answers on the fourth ring.

"Willie," she says, stopping for a few seconds to catch her breath. "I just got back from lunch. Sorry I'm a little short-winded."

Clara is the Prestwould's elder stateswoman. She's eighty-four, with a lively mind and a failing body. And, having spent much of her married life in Windsor Farms before moving to a condo after her husband's death, she knows some people.

"The Pratts? Chip and Page. A lovely couple. I knew his father too. I think Chip is Wilson Junior. I think . . . yes, that's right. Wilson Pratt Senior moved here from somewhere in the valley. Must have been forty years ago. I think he was commonwealth's attorney in one of those towns. He still goes to Saint James, and I think he lives with Chip and his family. But I don't believe they were at services this morning."

I explain why they might have skipped church today.

"Oh, my goodness," Clara says. "I'm glad I was sitting down when you told me that. But the little girl is OK?"

As far as I know, I tell her.

"Thank goodness for that. Anna is a lovely girl."

I get to the purpose of my call. I need to talk to the Pratts.

"Certainly," Clara says without hesitation. "I'll call the son and tell him that you are a fine reporter and one of my favorite people with hardly any criminal record. If that doesn't work, I guess you're on your own."

She says she'll call me back and tell me whether I'm welcome at the Pratts's or not.

I thank my old friend.

"Aw, Willie," she says before she rings off, "anything for you. It's too bad I didn't catch you thirty years ago, when I was in my prime."

While I'm waiting to hear from Clara, I call Marcus Green at home.

"Yeah, I figured that somehow I'd be hearing from you. Damn. Even white folks ain't safe anymore."

Marcus, who lives in a house just as nice as any of those in Windsor Farms but a couple of miles away, out in the county, loves to play the role of the street-savvy Black crusader, friend of the downtrodden.

I explain why I think Sylvester Simms needs a lawyer of his magnitude.

"Why don't you ever bring me a damn client that can pay?" Marcus complains.

The ones who wind up on the wrong side of justice, I explain to him, usually don't have a lot of money.

Marcus is married to my third ex-wife, Kate. I am Marcus Jr.'s godfather. It's a long story.

Marcus loves money, being a lawyer, but he also loves publicity, and he really does get off on scoring an upset win with an underdog client.

I tell him the latest twist and why Sly Simms's arrest might not be reason for Richmond to rest easy.

"So some nut with a knife tried to snatch a little girl?" he asks. "Damn.

"What you think about what that Pitts guy wrote this morning?" he asks.

Marcus knows there's some truth in today's epistle. He also knows, being a pragmatist, that this is how it is. And I know Marcus well enough to be sure that he'd defend some white drifter just as vigorously as he'd go to bat for blood kin, as long as he has a chance to win and he gets lots of ink.

We agree to talk tomorrow at his and Kate's office.

My phone starts beeping and I ring off with Marcus.

"Wilson Junior said he'd be willing to talk to you if you can come over in the next hour or so," Clara says.

I thank her. Then I call Cindy and tell her why I won't be home "just yet."

She knows that "just yet" is not a time frame that can be confined to minutes and hours. She sighs and hangs up.

✦ ✦ ✦

I FIND the Pratt abode on the first try this time.

Wilson "Chip" Pratt answers the door.

He has the look of a former jock, gone a little chunky with some gray in otherwise-brown hair. He's forty-six, according to the bio information I found earlier. None of the other Pratts seem to be available to me.

"Clara said you were OK," he says. "You've got to understand, we're all pretty damn shook up about this. Anna's going to be OK though. I think Page is more shook up than she is."

Chip Pratt is holding a glass of bourbon with a couple of melting ice cubes in it.

"Tough day," I observe.

He looks down at his drink and nods. He asks me if I want one. I lie and say "no."

We sit down in chairs on opposite sides of a very pricey-looking leather couch so we can remove our corona masks, and he gives me the details.

Anna, who's twelve, had spent the night with a friend who lives two blocks away. She was walking home "within eyesight of our damn house" when it happened.

"She said she heard a car coming up behind her, and she moved out of the street to let it pass. She said the woman who was driving called her over to ask directions. Anna was on the left side of the car, and she said that when she walked up to the window, which was tinted, the window rolled down, and she saw that the woman was wearing a ski mask."

"Wait. You said it was a woman?"

"Yeah, a woman."

The would-be abductor opened the door and grabbed Anna by the arm. The girl could see what she said was a "great big knife" in the woman's right hand.

"She said she tried to drag her into the car, but Anna's a pretty strong kid. The woman slashed at her with the knife, apparently, and nicked her arm. A couple of inches more . . ."

Chip stops talking long enough to gulp down most of the bourbon and get a grip.

"Anyhow, Anna said that the woman started to get out of the car, but then I guess she figured she couldn't catch her without drawing attention to herself. Anna said she was screaming by then, and the damn bitch drove off."

The girl was too rattled to remember much about the car, except that it was white and looked like maybe a Honda or a Toyota.

"My wife heard her screaming and went to the door, and here comes Anna, with blood running down her arm."

She couldn't tell the cops much about the woman in the car either.

"She said she thought she was tall, taller than her anyhow, and Anna's like five six. She said she thought her hair was blonde, but she couldn't tell much, because of the mask. She said she didn't say anything after she'd lured her over to the car."

Anna told her parents and the police that she thought the woman was "really old, like maybe even older than her mom and dad, but not as old as her granddad," Chip says.

I'm about to thank Pratt for his help when I hear a door open down the hall. A man who appears to be in his eighties comes shuffling toward us. Wilson Pratt Sr. introduces himself.

"I've seen some bad people in my time," he says, mentioning that, as Clara told me, he once was a commonwealth's attorney for one of the counties up in the valley, "but to attack a little girl like that. Do me a favor: Catch the piece of shit."

I advise the elder Pratt that I'm not a cop, just a reporter.

"Well, damn," he says. "Just do the best you can then."

As I'm walking down the brick walkway to the car, I look back and see a pair of twelve-year-old eyes peering at me from what must be an upstairs bedroom window.

I'm no shrink, but she doesn't look like she's exactly "OK" just yet.

✦ ✦ ✦

So back to the newsroom.

L.D., with no other choice, confirms what Chip Pratt told me: either there are two knife-wielding maniacs loose in Richmond or the cops have nailed the wrong damn guy.

"Either way," Sally Velez says, "tomorrow ought to be another big day for gun sales."

I write what I know, sure it'll be on the six o'clock TV news. My every instinct tells me to sit on this and post my story after ten so the first inkling people have of this will be when they pick up tomorrow morning's paper, but Sarah pretty much orders me to put it online now.

"We're not in the twentieth century anymore, Willie," she explains. "The TV folks will have to credit us, and even if you posted it late tonight, we'd put it online then anyhow."

Plus, she says, with common sense beyond her years, we need to let people know they still might want to watch their asses, as soon as possible.

Why, I wonder out loud, do we even print a newspaper?

"Don't let anybody from Grimm hear you say that," she advises.

It's been a hellish six days. Three people murdered and a twelve-year-old girl lucky not to be the fourth, apparently.

Is it possible the abduction today had nothing to do with those other two incidents? Anything's possible, but old Occam and his razor are telling me that three separate knife attacks on the apparently innocent in six days, maybe two miles apart, do not equal two different maniacs, and that the chump residing in the city jail right now is guilty of nothing worse than robbing a dead man.

I've already called Cindy again to tell her that I will be home for sure in time for supper. She says don't bother, that she, Abe, and Stella are going over to the Mellow Mushroom for pizza.

One more call before I pack it in.

Peachy answers on the fourth ring.

Yes, she was the one who told Sarah about the Pratt girl's near-abduction. No, she didn't tell Sarah who she was.

"I tried to call you," she says. "You didn't pick up, and I thought you all ought to know as soon as possible."

Never heard it ring in all the hubbub at Joe's. Like the rest of me, my ears ain't what they used to be.

CHAPTER SIX

Monday, January 11

THIS MORNING'S story on the botched abduction in Windsor Farms has, as expected, inflamed the populace.

There's a drive-time talk show on one of the local radio stations, and I sometimes listen to it to gauge the local temperature while I'm drinking my coffee and wishing for a cigarette.

The yakkers who call in this morning mostly want to talk about serial killers. The older ones remember some of the grislier cases in Richmond's past.

Some of them desire to share their opinions:

+ The woman in the car was an accomplice of the sap who's locked up, kind of like those two bastard snipers who terrorized everybody from DC to Richmond a few years ago.
+ She's a copycat slasher.
+ They're both part of some Satanic cult.
+ This has been going on for years and the cops have covered it up.

The only ones not weighing in directly on the murders phone to rag on or defend Marshall Pitts for claiming we are prejudiced against Black murder victims. Their opinions vary, from their voices, according to their racial backgrounds.

"Why do you listen to that crap?" Cindy asks as she refills my coffee mug.

"Those are our readers," I remind her.

"Better not piss anybody off today," she advises. "Everybody in Richmond's probably armed by now."

✦ ✦ ✦

WE'RE SUPPOSED to go to the movies today. I didn't expect to be able to safely sit in a theater for the foreseeable future, but Cindy maintains that there's a deluxe (read: expensive) movie palace out at one of the malls where you lounge in cushy rocking-chair seats, far away from the other patrons, and can eat something other than popcorn.

"They even let you order wine."

I ask if they have Miller tall necks. She says she doesn't think so. And, no, you can't smoke.

After my disappearing act yesterday, it would behoove me not to spend another alleged off day away from my beloved.

"We've got some pretty sharp knives here," she reminds me.

I do have an appointment with Marcus Green, I remind her.

"I've made reservations for a show at 2:10," Cindy says. "Be here by 1:30."

Marcus's office is just a few blocks down Franklin Street. It isn't a good morning for a walk, but this will save me from paying to park, slightly alleviating the damage to my wallet that a pricey movie is going to inflict.

I walk up in the bikes-only lane on Franklin that used to be open to cars. There are, as usual, no cyclists to dodge between the Prestwould and the spacious offices of Green & Ellis. It's a one-Camel walk.

Marcus and Kate are both in. I stop by to say hello to ex-wife No. 3.

"Have you sent the check yet?" Kate asks.

She means the one for the rent.

"No," I tell her. "We just can't scrape the money together right now. Maybe later."

We're bullshitting each other. It strikes me that we laugh at the same thing once in a while now, as we didn't do in the frosty autumn of our marriage.

I should be happy that rent's the only thing I owe Kate, other than an apology for being a lousy husband. She's earning multiples of what I make now. Hell, I should ask her for alimony.

She shows me a picture of Marcus Jr., who she says is on the verge of walking.

"Maybe we should've had one of those," I suggest.

Her look says, "Don't go there."

Marcus comes out, chewing on a donut.

"You ready to roll?"

I appreciated his letting me accompany him on this getting-to-know-you visit with Sly Simms. I also appreciate the fact that he's even willing to consider a client who will have to pay for his services with recycled beer cans.

"I haven't decided to take him on yet," Marcus says.

He agrees that the attempted abduction or murder or whatever the woman had in mind yesterday makes Mr. Simms's culpability in those three killings questionable at best.

I've already filled my lawyer pal in on Simms's mental capacity, as related to me by Awesome Dude.

"Awesome says the guy isn't what you'd call extremely mentally competent."

Marcus chuckles.

"Pot calling the kettle black."

We get to the jail, over on the other side of I-95, a little before ten. There's a little pushback about me accompanying Marcus, but they finally let us both in.

We get our first view at Sylvester Simms ten minutes later. The picture we ran in the paper didn't look much worse than the individual who is led into the interview room, his ankles and wrists shackled.

He is as weather-beaten as an abandoned row house, and if he really weighs 120 pounds, I'd be surprised. One eye is swollen shut, and there's dried blood on his upper lip. The jailer, Marcus, and I tower over him. He looks like somebody who's used to being beaten and just takes it.

"Who did this to you?" Marcus asks after Simms sits down in the metal folding chair across the table from us.

The man shrugs his shoulders.

A few more questions make me believe he honest-to-God doesn't know. The light behind his one good eye is pretty damn dim. Could have been the cops. Could have been another inmate. Sly Simms is obviously accustomed to being somebody's punching bag.

We've both read the details: Simms was apprehended in the parking lot of a dicey convenience store. He had a dead man's VISA card and watch in his possession. After a few hours of heart-to-heart with some of L.D.'s detectives, he remembered a lot of things.

He remembered killing that poor sucker, plundering his wallet, and dumping his body over by the river. He remembered breaking into the house in Westover Hills and killing those two people. I have a feeling that if the dicks had pushed it, they could have made him remember kidnapping the Lindbergh baby.

"What did you do with the knife?" Marcus asks him.

"I dunno."

We know that this was one thing the cops weren't able to pin down. The murder weapon, and it appears from forensic evidence that the same type was used on Bell and the McCaskills, has not been found. No amount of police persuasion could get that tidbit of information out of the alleged perp.

"Do you even own a knife?" Marcus asks.

A shrug.

"I don't think so. They said I did, but I don't remember no knife."

He is more lucid when we get him talking about the one thing he definitely did do. He says he was walking over by the river when he found what turned out to be Harlan Bell's body.

"And you took his watch and went through his wallet and took his charge card?"

Simms shrugs.

"He wasn't gonna need it."

"Didn't you know they'd catch you?" Marcus asks. "The man's name is on the card."

"I always thought it'd be cool to have one of them cards," Simms says. "Never had one before. Didn't work so good though."

The sense of resignation is what strikes me. There might not have been a more willing confessor in the city of Richmond than Sylvester Simms.

"I need to know something," Marcus says, "and I need the truth. Did you kill those people?"

He keeps his head down, avoiding eye contact.

"They say I did, so I must of."

"But you don't remember?"

"I have some trouble, remembering stuff, since the accident."

I wonder how in God's name the cops or the prosecutor think any jury can be convinced that this guy was able and willing to plan and carry out the killing of three people.

Of course, it'll never come to that, unless Simms has a real lawyer. There'll either be a plea bargain or he'll be shipped off to Central State as mentally incompetent.

With a court-appointed attorney, it would be very easy to wipe this one off the books and put Sylvester Simms out of sight, out of mind.

A combination of that botched attack yesterday and Marcus Green's not insubstantial talents is going to make it damn hard for that scenario to play out now. This one is going to bite both the chief and the mayor on the butt, it says here.

It takes Marcus less than an hour to decide to take Simms's case. The suspect doesn't seem to really know what's going on, but he appears to appreciate that neither of us seems very likely to hit him.

"If you have any trouble, if anybody bothers you, you let me know," Marcus says.

Sly smiles for the first time, not a pretty sight.

"Thank you," he says. He says it like he hasn't had reason to thank anybody for anything for a long time.

✦ ✦ ✦

There's time to go by the newsroom and bang out a few hundred words about Sylvester Simms, including the fact that he now has a lawyer of some repute on his side. I don't come right out and say that the cops blew it, but a normally intelligent person, or even a smart Labrador retriever, could figure it out, especially coming on the heels of that attack yesterday.

Wheelie and Sarah both read what I wrote before I dash home in time to make my movie deadline.

"So this guy is really as, um, mentally challenged as he seems?" Wheelie asks.

"I think the medical terminology is 'one beer short of a six-pack.'"

I've summarized what the Pratt girl's father told me yesterday. I've also checked in with L.D.

"Didn't I tell you those people didn't want to talk to you?" the chief asks when I call him. He asks it loud enough to hurt my bad ear.

"Seemed to me like they were fine with it," I reply.

I ask him whether he really thought Richmond's finest had nabbed the right psychopath.

"He confessed. What the hell else do you need? That woman yesterday, maybe she was a copycat, inspired, I might add, by your goddamn muckraking articles."

That's when I told L.D. that this new candidate for killer-at-large is not the only problem he might be facing.

"He's got a lawyer now," I inform the chief.

When I tell him who it is, he curses for a few seconds before he hangs up.

Sally Velez was sitting close enough to me that she could hear most of what L.D. was saying.

"Sure hope you don't need any parking tickets fixed anytime soon," she says.

✦ ✦ ✦

I GET home at 1:27. Cindy seems surprised that I made good on my promise. Oh, ye of little faith.

"That's good," she says as she goes to put on her coat. "Now I don't have to change the locks on the doors."

We get to the cinema in time to order beer and wine to take to our cushy seats. The movie wasn't that bad, although nothing blew up and there was only minimal potty humor. The sandwich and fries didn't suck, not great, but what the hell do you expect in a damn movie theater? We did slip the masks off when the lights went down, scofflaws that we are.

My fourth bride and I coexist as well as most, I suppose. She does the *New York Times* Sunday crossword while I watch pro football, and then I pretend to care about whatever the fuck is on *Masterpiece Theater.*

"What language are they speaking?" I asked last night.

She shook her head.

"English."

"Sort of," I conceded.

On the way back from the movie, we take the scenic route and drive down Monument Avenue, which is conspicuously devoid of monuments these days. J.E.B. Stuart, Stonewall Jackson, Matthew Fontaine Maury, and Jefferson Davis are gone, toppled last year when Black Lives Matter turned into another Confederate bloodbath. Only Robert E. Lee survives, at least until the courts decide what the city is allowed to do with him.

As we are returning to our humble digs, we unfortunately run into Feldman, aka McGrumpy around the Prestwould, in the lobby.

"Did they catch her yet?" he asks, and I deduce that he's talking about whoever tried to hurt little Anna Pratt yesterday.

I explain that I haven't checked with anyone at the paper in a few hours, but I'm sure that the cops are all over it.

"Well, they need to get off their butts and find that bitch," McGrumpy says, then goes on to grumble about how there's almost no security at all in our building. We used to have a guard staying all night in the lobby, but Feldman and others decided to knock a few bucks off their ruinous condo fees and do away with that amenity.

"Maybe we could pay that big Indian a few bucks to stay down here at night," he says.

He means Custalow, of course. I explain, patiently as I can, that Abe is the head maintenance guy and is already putting in closer to fifty than forty hours a week.

"I hope we're not paying him overtime," McGrumpy grumps. Cindy gently prods me with her elbow, meaning it's time to leave before I wrap my hands around Feldman's chicken neck and start squeezing.

As we're waiting for the elevator, the old coot reaches into his coat pocket and pulls out a pistol.

"Put that thing down, you idiot," I advise.

"Nobody's going to cut my throat, no sir," he says, putting the weapon back in his pocket.

If Feldman, whose age and weight are approaching ninety from different directions, has bought a fucking gun, it means everybody in town indeed must be armed.

✦ ✦ ✦

PEOPLE WHO said they'd never take the COVID shot are trying to figure out how to jump the line and get it now. Cindy says that anybody who eats at McDonald's has no reason to complain about having control over what they put in their bodies.

"That train," she says, "has already left the station."

"Certainly," she said to me the other day, "a vaccine can't be as bad for you as Camels."

Hell, I'm all for it, but I'd like to see people who really need it, like Peggy and Awesome, get it first.

I check in at the paper. Sarah says there's no news from the police about yesterday's attack.

"There are a lot of white Toyotas and Hondas out there, if it even is one of those, and nobody much is out on the streets in that neighborhood."

As in some of our less-wealthy enclaves, nobody saw nothin'.

About six thirty, I call Peachy at home to see if she can tell me anything that L.D. Jones would prefer she didn't.

"Nothing so far, Willie. The little girl had a decent description, but nothing's shown up so far. Man, the chief is really pissed about this whole thing. You know how much he hates to be wrong."

Yeah, I'm sure there will be some kind of press release coming out soon from the mayor's office putting all the blame on the police for nabbing the wrong culprit.

Hell, I can't blame L.D. or his minions that much for jumping to conclusions. I mean, you catch a guy at the Grab 'n' Go wearing a dead man's watch, and you figure, case solved.

Where they screwed up, though, was in getting a little overeager in wringing out a confession from a guy who, from what I saw, couldn't swear to you what day it was. If Marcus Green has anything to do with it, and he does, Sylvester Simms might have a little walking-around money, compliments of the city, when he's allowed to walk around again.

I tell Sarah that I don't have anything else for the Tuesday paper, but add that we're going to be flogging this one for some time to come.

"Well," she says, "busy hands are employed hands."

I get her drift. There aren't many of us left to lay off, but the Grimm Group probably hasn't squeezed all the blood out of this turnip yet.

"How should I turn in my overtime for today?" I ask.

She laughs.

"The same way you always do. With invisible ink."

CHAPTER SEVEN

Tuesday, January 12

AWESOME DUDE might not be the most reliable source on the planet. A lifetime of recreational drug use has served to blur the lines between reality and perception inside his addled head.

However he does know some shit. I always listen when he wants to talk, because sometimes he has something to say.

An old reporter, as in almost as old as I am now, taught me a lesson a long time ago. Fawcett was working for the afternoon paper, back when the Earth's crust had not yet cooled and cities the size of Richmond had the luxury of two daily newspapers. He was the competition, and we were both covering the legislature.

There was an ancient coot, a political groupie, who hung around the capitol, and he was always trying to give me some kind of "hot tip" about various malfeasances he said our elected representatives were committing.

I checked out a couple of them, and all I did was waste my time. So I stopped listening when Chubbs sidled up to me.

One day, he pulled me aside with a big scoop about a state senator who was considering a run for governor.

"He said he was an All-American linebacker for Kansas," Chubbs said, almost whispering it to me as I rushed from one hearing to another. "He's lying."

The guy did have it on his résumé that he was a former college football star. Then he went to law school and eventually turned up in Virginia, where he managed to get himself elected to feed at the state trough.

I just nodded my head and told Chubbs I had to be somewhere for a meeting.

Two days later, Fawcett broke the story in the afternoon paper that the would-be governor had never played a down for the Kansas varsity or anybody else's varsity. He'd been a walk-on on the freshman team and didn't last a season there. It kind of killed his higher ambitions.

My editor wanted to know why the fuck I didn't have that story before Fawcett did. The readers don't give two shits about who breaks a story first, but reporters and their bosses do.

Fawcett was not a bad guy, just the competition. He and I had drinks together from time to time.

Two days after the story broke, I ran into him at a watering hole favored by the pols and hangers-on.

"Chubbs said he told you about our legislative All-American," he said after we'd had a couple of drinks. "Said you didn't seem too interested."

I observed that Chubbs was often full of crap.

"Yeah," Fawcett said, "he is that. But you've got to know that even a stopped clock is right a couple of times a day."

After that, whenever Chubbs grabbed me with the promise of a hot tip, I listened. And, like Fawcett said, once or twice he was right. That was worth all the times he was wrong.

And so, being capable of eventual growth, I made it a point to listen to the blowhards, the self-important peddlers of rumors, and the intellectually impaired.

Thus, when Peggy calls this morning, interrupting my breakfast, and says Awesome Dude has some important information, I make a trip over to Laurel Street.

"I heard something about ol' Sly," he tells me after my old mom has made me a cup of coffee.

Awesome is the only person who has spent time with Sylvester Simms. I let the ears work.

There is another man, equally as destitute as Mr. Simms, who told Awesome he had been with him holed up in somebody's garage in the Fan, the night the McCaskills were murdered.

"He's sure it was the same night."

"Last Thursday. Yeah, he's sure. He said it was the night before that church bunch feeds everybody over at the park, on Friday. They walked over there the next morning."

Awesome's source says they were there all night, warding off the winter chill with a couple of bottles of cheap wine that Sly had somehow been able to buy.

"Do you know where this guy is? Or what his name is?"

The Dude is not exactly sure. He knows the man by what's probably his first name, Diego, "but Diego moves around a lot. He don't have no fixed address. I think he's Mexican or something."

Awesome says he'll try to find Diego again. I thank him for the information.

"Aw, anything for you, Willie," he says, showing a grin that suffers from the kind of dental care you get when you have no fixed address. He has one now, but, tooth-wise, the damage has been done.

I pass this information on to Marcus Green. There's nothing to write at present. As much as I respect Awesome, information relayed from some homeless guy, last name unknown, to Awesome Dude to me is a bridge too far. But maybe Marcus can shake some trees and see what falls out.

He thanks me, tepidly, and says he'll check into it.

"My new client," he says, "is starting to look more innocent all the time."

"Well," I tell him, "I'm sure you'll see that justice gets done."

I wonder sometimes if Marcus is a fanatic about justice, but he does like to win.

I drop by police headquarters. L.D. is in his office. As usual, he has instructed his aide to make sure I am kept at arm's length. I convince the aide that I'm going to run a story with a reliable source vouching for Sly Simms's whereabouts the night the McCaskills were killed, and that it would be good to get a response from the chief.

She frowns but gets up from her desk and walks into the chief's inner sanctum, closing the door behind her.

She's back momentarily.

"OK," she says, somewhat grudgingly. "He says you can go in, but just for a minute."

"You are," L.D. says, "the biggest pain in the ass in the city of Richmond. Why don't you die or something?"

I tell him I'm working on it.

The chief is less than impressed about the reliability of my reliable source.

"You interrupted my busy day to tell me something one drug-addled individual heard from another drug-addled individual, this Diego character, and nobody even knows the guy's last name? Get the fuck out of here, Willie. If you think this means anything, then go ahead and write it. I dare you."

I tell him that I'm not writing anything until I can get it confirmed, hopefully by finding Diego. I mention that I give this some credence because of the attack on the Pratt girl two days ago, and that I'm dead certain Marcus Green also is looking for Diego.

"Look," L.D. says, "we're trying to find that woman, whoever she is, but in the meantime, we aren't about to turn this Simms character loose. Hell, we know he stole shit off the body of a dead man. That's enough to hold him until we get this sorted out."

"It might bite you in the ass," I warn him.

He sighs. The chief doesn't sigh a lot. He is much fonder of active forms of aggression.

"Willie," he says. "Shut the door."

He means "from the inside," an unusual move for a man who is normally glad to see me close it from the other side, on the way out of his hair.

"This is off the record," he says.

I agree, but am not totally comfortable with it. Whatever he tells me now, I won't be able to print, which means some other asshole might get it before I do, on the record. But, hell, there's so little competition in the news business these days that my fears are, on a scale of 1 to 10, about a 2.

What L.D. needs me to know is this: Our mayor is going to announce, very soon, that he is running for the Democratic nomination for lieutenant governor, putting him maybe one term away from the governor's mansion.

"Hell, he might get it," the chief says. "But the thing is, he doesn't want any negative news upsetting his fuckin' apple cart right now."

He doesn't need any breaking stories about his police department arresting the wrong man in what has become at least a regionally interesting serial-killer story.

"It's gonna eat him up later," I say, "if you really do have the wrong perp and the right one's still on the loose."

"Fuck, I know that. But he doesn't see it that way. He doesn't want to hear anything but 'case closed' right now."

L.D. shakes his head.

"If it was up to me, I might go in a different direction here. But I am under orders—and this is definitely double-secret off the record, Willie—to tell the world we're sure this Simms character is our man."

I observe that it won't be just the chief eating dirt if Simms turns out to be innocent of murder.

He almost smiles.

"It's always a good thing to cover your butt around here, Willie," he says.

It turns out that the mayor, when he ordered L.D. to focus on the serial killer he's already arrested, was being recorded.

"He told me that if he ever caught me taping his ass again, nothing would save me," the chief says. "But he didn't say anything about an eyewitness, or rather an earwitness."

The chief saved his job last year after the Black Lives Matter unrest when he recorded the mayor saying some things Hizzoner wishes he'd never said.

This time, L.D. turned to Jimbo Stefanski, his number two guy. When he called the mayor to wonder whether Sylvester Simms was indeed a serial killer, the chief made sure Stefanski was standing right there by the speaker phone. The mayor told L.D. that it would be in his best interests to keep Sly right where he is.

"And then he spilled the beans."

He told the chief, and inadvertently Jimbo Stefanski, that he was days away from announcing his run at the lieutenant governor nomination.

"And he said, and I quote, 'I don't want anything screwing that up.'"

Jimbo was taking notes. He typed them up afterward, and he and the chief both signed a letter spelling out their misgivings.

"So, if this all blows up, it's going to be in the mayor's face and not yours."

L.D. shrugs.

"He lit the fuse."

It has long amazed me how little competency one has to exhibit to get elected mayor or even governor. I used to cover the state legislature, before I fucked that up, and I saw a lot of stupid. The mayor, if he can manage to slip through this dumpster fire without third-degree burns, should feel right at home.

In the meantime, the chief assures me that he is not in the least convinced that Sly Simms is a serial killer.

"Just give me a few days," he says. "We're gonna keep searching for that woman, mayor be damned. He doesn't have to know everything. In the meantime, Simms can sit tight. He's going to jail anyhow, for stealing that charge card, but at least he can probably get bond then."

So we leave it at that.

One of the worst things a reporter can be is a confidant. A confidant knows everything but can't write any of it, because if he didn't promise his source that he wouldn't write what he knew, the source would freeze him out.

That's the pickle I'm in right now. Hopefully I won't be reading about the mayor's political ambitions in the *Washington Post* or the local alternative weekly.

In the meantime, I'm using my spare time before reporting to the newsroom to talk to Mrs. Dorothy Bell.

She lives on Springhill Avenue, about a block from one of Dogtown's parks. I decide that it's better if I see her in person.

The neighborhood's middle class, like a location in a movie set in the 1960s. People who live in places like this should never have to deal with loved ones being butchered, but then again, nobody should have to deal with that.

A man in his thirties, whom I discover is her and the late Harlan Bell's son, answers the door. He is less than enthused about letting me speak with his mother, but she comes to the door and tells him it's OK.

Pretty much every flat surface is holding food, the best way friends and neighbors of the Bells knew to show their sympathy.

Mrs. Bell tries to get me to fix myself a plate. I thank her and decline.

We take off our masks and sit across a table of fried chicken, potato salad, and three different kinds of casserole.

She talks about "the arrangements," and how hard it is that she can't even have a decent memorial service until "this mess" is over and people can congregate again. I nod and listen.

I get some home-boy points by revealing that her late husband and I are both graduates of the mean streets of Oregon Hill. Perhaps I overinflate the depth of our boyhood relationship.

Finally I cut to the chase, after offering sympathy that is as heartfelt as is possible considering that I don't know Mrs. Bell.

"I guess you heard about the attack over in Windsor Farms Sunday."

She nods her head.

"That poor girl," she says. "But she was lucky, wasn't she?"

I tell Dorothy Bell that the fact that somebody attacked the girl much in the same way that her husband was attacked made me wonder if the man in jail is guilty.

"But he had Harlan's charge card, and his watch," she says.

I agree that that looks pretty bad, but that I've talked to Sylvester Simms, and he said he found Harlan Bell already dead and took what he could. I also opine on Simms's apparent mental capability.

"He's going to jail, no doubt, but that attack on Sunday has got me wondering."

Mrs. Bell has one very cogent question.

"Are the police wondering, too, or is it just you?"

I assure her that the police are trying very hard to find the woman who did the attack on Sunday, even if they won't admit it.

"In the meantime," I press on, "I just wonder: Why? Your husband sounds like he was a wonderful man. What could have made somebody do what they did last Tuesday?"

She shakes her head.

"Believe me, I've asked myself that over and over, and it doesn't make any sense at all. You couldn't find a person on this planet who had anything against Harlan. I mean, there was the occasional misunderstanding about a plumbing bill, but nothing that didn't end on a friendly note. Harlan tried to work with people."

Her son has come into the living room. He's frowning at me like he thinks it's time for me to stop pestering his mourning mother.

Dorothy Bell assures her watchful offspring that she's fine.

"I just don't want people bothering you," he says, looking at me.

In an effort to convince him that I am not the devil, I repeat my earnest desire to report the truth.

He snorts.

"Yeah. You just want a story for your damn newspaper."

His mother admonishes him for his foul language.

Then she turns back to me.

"This is silly," she says, "but the only time in my life I ever saw anybody mad at Harlan Bell was, my goodness, must have been thirty-two, thirty-three years ago."

As she relates it, the Bells were living in a small town up in the valley, near Staunton.

"It was the year you were born," she says to her son. "Nineteen eight-eight."

Bell had been doing some work at some rich guy's house out in the country. Shortly afterward, the guy and his wife were murdered.

"It was terrible, from what I heard. The police said their own daughter did it. Harlan was called as a witness, because he had seen the daughter in a violent argument with her parents. He said she even threatened to kill them. He said later he wished he'd never even told the police about it, because it got him right in the middle of things."

At the trial, he testified to what he had seen and heard.

"But when he stepped down, Harlan said the daughter started screaming and cursing at him, calling him a liar and making all sorts of threats before they had to remove her from the courtroom. She got close enough to him to spit on him.

"He said he'd never seen anybody so mad."

She sighs.

"But that was more than thirty years ago. Don't even know why I mentioned it. I mean, he never heard from her after that. I don't even remember the girl's name.

"Anyhow," she says, trying to work up a smile, "that's the last time I ever heard of anybody being mad at Harlan Bell."

I remark that that's a pretty good record. Hell, I've often managed to piss off multiple people in the same day.

I ask if Mrs. Bell has had her COVID vaccine shot yet, just to make conversation.

"No," she says. "I'm just not up for trying very hard right now. Maybe the Lord will take me too."

✦ ✦ ✦

I PICK up a pastrami and Swiss on toasted rye at Perly's and drive the three blocks to the paper.

Apparently I just missed the big excitement of the day there.

The sports department recently hired a part-timer to cover some of the stuff we used to be able to cover ourselves before our corporate masters neutered us. Most of our part-timers are college kids looking to get a foot in the door of a dying industry's old folks' home for some damn reason.

This one didn't fit the profile. He was a retired teacher who thought it would be fun to go to high school ball games for free and write about them. Go figure.

When HR interviews people who want to work here, I guess they don't ask, "Are you an anti-vaxxer?"

It's become a problem all around town. We've had a few stories about people refusing to wear masks duking it out with people who take offense at that.

Today those lucky few who were in the newsroom at the time got a front-row seat in real time.

The new hire, who turned out to be sixty-six years old, had come in to write a feature about one of our high school phenoms. Mostly we like for our part-timers and many of our full-timers to work at home, allegedly for safety concerns but maybe just to save electricity.

At any rate, he wasn't wearing a mask.

Bootie Carmichael, who wandered in to write a column on the University of Virginia's unexpectedly competent basketball team, told him to put one on.

Bootie's not usually a stickler for following the rules, but he's older than the man without the mask and about sixty pounds overweight, so I guess he feels like people refusing to wear masks are trying to kill him.

The guy said he didn't have a mask. He also said that the whole plan to require them was "a pack of lies."

Bootie told him to get his ass out of the newsroom if he insisted on putting Bootie's health at risk. The guy's two-word answer, reportedly, was "Make me."

So Bootie did. Sally said she didn't know our aged, booze-soaked sports columnist could move so fast. He apparently picked the guy up, threw him over his shoulder and carried him across the newsroom to the elevators, where he deposited him inside and punched "1."

He advised the guy to get the fuck out and not come back. So far he hasn't.

He then went back to his desk and called our latest sports editor, here almost two years now, and told him he was going to need to hire another part-timer.

I dropped by Bootie's desk and congratulated him on a job well done.

"It'd be a hell of a note," the old-timer said, wheezing a little as he said it, "if I had a heart attack trying to stay healthy."

✦ ✦ ✦

I DON'T have anything much to add for Wednesday's paper, but it's three P.M., and the night cops beat awaits me. Odds are, I'll have some mayhem to report between now and midnight.

I feel for Mrs. Bell, but she didn't tell me much I didn't know already. Maybe, if I have time tonight, I'll look into that long-ago murder trial she mentioned. Fool's errands are my specialty.

CHAPTER EIGHT

Wednesday, January 13

LAST NIGHT kept me busy. First, the cops found a young woman's body in a car near Ladies Mile Road. She'd been missing for almost a month, and Peachy said the police figured her body had been in the car, abandoned at the edge of a small park, for at least a week. She said her remains were in the back seat, covered by a blanket.

"And nobody noticed?"

"Nobody that was willing to call 911."

It depresses me to think that a human being could lie dead and ignored in a car that was hard by a public park for a week or more. I wish this was a unique case in our fair city.

"Cause of death?"

"She wasn't shot or otherwise assaulted, as far as they can tell. That's all they know. Maybe she froze to death."

No knife wounds, I'm assured.

Then, about eleven, too late to make our new, improved deadlines, there was an apparent road-rage shooting out on I-95, within eyesight of the VCU Medical Center, our big teaching hospital.

I got over to the emergency room entrance and was able to schmooze my way inside, where the family of the wounded man was waiting.

A woman who identified herself as his wife said she and the victim were coming home from a joint in the Bottom when an SUV started tailgating them.

Her husband "might have" given an inappropriate hand signal to the driver behind them, she said, "but that didn't give him no cause to shoot him."

She was able to give a pretty good ID of the SUV, even part of the license plate number, so it's a good bet that Mr. Red-ass will be behind bars soon.

Cindy's always after me about not suffering automotive fools gladly when we're out together. Some of them, she reminds me, are armed. Statistics tell us there is about one gun per human in the commonwealth.

Maybe I should listen to her.

When I learned that the shooting victim would live, according to what the ER doctor told the family, I punched out a few grafs for our online audience. Everybody has a car. Everybody's been mad enough to give the finger to some jackass with subpar driving manners. People can relate, and maybe even learn.

✦ ✦ ✦

TODAY I have it on my to-do list to talk to someone who was close to the couple who were murdered over in Westover Hills. Last night I discovered that they have a grown son living in the Museum District. I have an address.

It's after ten when I get there, and no one's home. I thought he might be off work still, dealing with what one has to deal with when one's parents are murdered.

He's employed by one of the brokerage firms downtown. I decide not to leave a note on the door and plan to try and catch up with him after six.

Sarah Goodnight calls me as I'm driving away from the McCaskill son's townhouse.

"The mayor's called a press conference," she tells me. Leighton Byrd has already left for City Hall, but Sarah thought I should go, too, "in case it has something to do with the killings."

I have a sinking feeling that it has nothing to do with the killings and everything to do with Hizzoner's higher ambitions.

When I get there, a handful of TV reporters and cameramen are already in place.

Leighton comes out when she sees me.

"Know anything about this?" she asks.

I profess complete ignorance. The only thing worse than sitting on a story and having it scorch your ass when it blows up is having junior confederates know that you knew and didn't share with our readers.

The mayor comes out, looking fine in his thousand-dollar suit and hundred-dollar haircut, and tells the assembled what they could have read in this morning's paper if I hadn't promised to keep it to myself.

Yes, indeed. Our leader is running for lieutenant governor.

He says all the usual things: We need fresh blood. It's a new day for Virginia. Social progressivism twinned with a fiscal conservativism—like those two are going to coexist. Better health care, but no new taxes. Unicorns and rainbows.

Leighton's not yet twenty-five, but she's old enough to have a bullshit detector.

"Does he really believe that crap?" she whispers.

It doesn't matter if he believes it or not, I reply, sotto voce. He just has to get enough voters to believe it, or at least think he's lying less than the other candidates.

The real bottom line will be who gets the most campaign donations. The day after the election in November,

anyone who can count can compare campaign contributions with votes and see how loud money talks.

The other people angling for the Democratic nomination probably are at least as ambitious and morally ambivalent as Hizzoner. It's just that I don't know the others as
well.

L.D. Jones is standing a few feet away.

I see him smile and shake his head as the mayor makes
his case.

He starts to walk toward us, and I'm guessing he's
going to apologize for gagging me. I look toward Leighton,
then make eye contact with the chief and shake my head.

"What?" she says, but L.D. understands. We'll talk later.

"Sometimes," she says as the press conference breaks
up and we walk away, "I think you're keeping shit from me."

"Perish the thought."

✦ ✦ ✦

I HAVE little to contribute to Leighton's story, so I head
for the Bamboo Café for a late breakfast or early lunch.
Three scrambled eggs, country ham, hash browns, English
muffin, and a four-dollar Bloody Mary. Maybe I'm too pre-
dictable. The waitress doesn't even give me a menu anymore. Cindy says I ought to carry a defibrillator around
with me for "when, not if, you keel over."

I'm about to order my second bloody when my phone
buzzes in my pocket.

It's Cindy, who's Zoom-teaching from home today.

"Just wanted you to know," she says. "The Garlands
have got it."

We all know what "it" is. We've only had one case of
COVID in the Prestwould until now. At least, that's all that
we know of. Some people think telling folks that they're
infected is like admitting to a moral failure. I'm an expert

on moral failures, and catching an airborne virus ain't one of them. When Peggy and Awesome got it last year, Andi and I sweated bullets until they survived it, but we didn't think they were somehow to blame. Marijuana does not, to my scant medical knowledge, cause COVID.

I tell my beloved to spray the elevator buttons, since Patti and Pete live right across the hall from us and share the same lift.

I call L.D. and he unexpectedly takes my call, I'm thinking either out of guilt or gratitude.

"Sorry that you didn't get the break on the mayor's announcement," he says.

He confirms what Marcus Green emailed me. Sly Simms is still locked up.

"Any sign of that woman who tried to abduct the Pratt girl?"

"Nothin' so far, but we're definitely looking."

It's been three days since that incident. I'm thinking but not saying that the cops would be putting on more of a full-court press if they didn't already have their alleged serial killer locked up.

"I wonder if maybe the girl didn't make it up," the chief says.

This is news to me.

"Were you there?" I ask. "Did she seem like she was making it up? Plus she did have a cut on her arm."

"Wasn't much more than a scratch."

"So you're just going to let this one die a slow, quiet death?"

"Dammit, Willie, I didn't say that. The mayor wants this one tied up, but we're looking. You do have to wonder though."

There isn't much left to say.

"Don't forget that you owe me one, after I dummied up about the mayor running for lieutenant governor."

L.D. snorts.

"I don't owe you shit."

So much for guilt and gratitude.

✦ ✦ ✦

I RUN by the newsroom. Leighton's already written the story on Hizzoner's political ambitions.

"Do you think he has a chance?" she asks.

He wouldn't be the first Richmond mayor to win a statewide election, I observe. One of our present US senators used to be our municipal leader.

It might be a good time to give Leighton a little insight into the mayor's true character. The story about how he suspended the chief last year after the Black Lives Matter upheaval and then had to bring him back to save his own duplicitous ass probably would give her an accurate snapshot. However I did promise L.D. that I wouldn't reveal that particular piece of blackmail.

I need to stop making promises.

If it turns out that the cops have the wrong man in jail and there's still a serial nut-job out there, and the mayor starts lining the chief up for another firing squad, L.D. has the ammo to blow him out of the water.

One thing I'm sure of: We aren't done with this case just yet.

Marshall Pitts had doubled down on his assertions that we're only paying so much attention to the three Dogtown murders because the victims were white. His column today has brought out the "I'm not a racist, but . . ." crowd.

Pitts looks a little stressed out when I walk by his desk.

I don't totally agree with Marshall on this one, but he and I both know that you don't lose readers by offending them so much as you do by boring them to death. Marshall is definitely not boring them.

I tell him to keep the faith. He seems surprised to receive kind words from me.

He shakes his head.

"Some son of a bitch left a watermelon on my front steps," he says, "with my name and 'KKK' painted on it."

"You have your next column," I advise.

"Fuckin' A," he says.

✦ ✦ ✦

I WORK on a story on the city's murder rate so far this year and file it. Then I explain to Sally Velez that I'm going to be gone for a couple of hours, between five and seven.

"You still think they've got the wrong guy locked up?"

I recount some of the reasons why I'm dubious. The attempted assault in Windsor Farms after Simms was locked up. The mysterious Diego who swears Sly was with him at the time the McCaskills were murdered. The firm belief, after talking to Sylvester Simms, that he had neither the will nor the brains to pull off a single and double execution.

"Well," Sally says, "just be sure you're back here by seven. I got nobody else for night cops."

As I'm leaving, she says, "By the way, have you heard about the dogs?"

Always happy to hear a good dog story, I postpone my departure.

The dogs belong to Weather Guy. In the midst of laying off scads of good, honest reporters, editors, and photographers a while back, the Grimm Group approved the hiring of a weather reporter. Guy Flowers does a good enough job, I guess, but in my opinion, we needed another body covering city council and the schools more than we needed a print version of those happy faces that tell you the temperature three times in half an hour on TV.

Weather Guy apparently had an inspiration recently.

One of the TV meteorologists has this Labrador retriever who is usually on camera with him at showtime. The dog rolls around in the grass, drinks from his dish, licks himself, or waits for the TV weatherman to give him another treat. The viewers love it. The Lab is probably the most popular individual on the six o'clock news.

So Weather Guy figured, if one Lab's a draw, why not two? Flowers does video for our website, and he wasn't getting a lot of views. So he adopted two retrievers. Actually he's borrowing them from a couple of dog-loving friends.

"When you go to the website," Sally says, "there he is, hamming it up and trying to control these two mutts, neither of which looks like it really wants to be there."

Starting tomorrow, his photo that goes with his weather column in the paper will be of him and his beloved, borrowed canines.

He brought them into the newsroom earlier today. Some of the staff made quite a to-do over them until they found out one of them wasn't completely toilet trained.

Hell, if Labrador retrievers can somehow make people buy newspapers again, or at least pay to access the website, release the hounds.

I promise Sally I'll be back before she knows it. She seems to doubt that.

✦ ✦ ✦

THERE'S A light on in Kevin McCaskill's place when I walk up for the second time today.

He answers my knock with a Scotch in hand.

I explain who I am and that I'm just doing a follow-up on his parents' murder, spouting some bullshit about wanting to give the victims at least as much exposure as we give the perps.

He puts his hand on the door frame, thinks about it for a few seconds, then says, "Sure, come on in."

He says he's divorced, with a couple of kids living in the Norfolk area with their mother.

"They moved here to be close to the grandkids," he says, "but then the marriage went to shit and Megan took the kids and moved to the beach."

McCaskill has a son who's thirteen and a daughter who's eleven.

"I could've moved down there, too, but I figured I'd stay here and kind of keep an eye on my folks."

He sighs, and then there's a catch in his voice when he says, "Apparently I didn't do a very good job of that."

He offers me a drink. I want to, but I'm afraid if Sally smells liquor on my breath when I return, bad things could happen.

After a while, I get him talking about his mom and dad.

"They were great. I couldn't have had better parents. Growing up, they were always the ones letting my and my sister's friends sleep over, fixing dinner and breakfast for everybody. It made me popular just being their son. It seemed like half of Staunton slept over at our place at least a time or two."

I had forgotten that the McCaskills were from Staunton.

I ask the obvious question.

"Did your folks know Harlan Bell?"

He looks puzzled.

"Who?"

I explain that Bell was the other alleged victim of Sylvester Simms.

He shakes his head.

"Uh, no. I don't think so. The guy was a plumber, right? My dad was a banker, so they probably didn't cross paths, unless he did some work for my folks."

Kevin McCaskill asks the obvious question.

"If they've already got this guy locked up, why are we even having this conversation?"

I explain my misgivings about Simms's guilt.

"Yeah, I saw the story about the girl over in Windsor Farms. Hell, I know her father from the Commonwealth Club. But you think whoever did that might have had something to do with what happened . . . ? Jesus. Are the cops all over this? I mean, the guy's still in jail, right?"

For now, I assure him.

I tell him I'm sorry for being such a nosy bastard.

He gets up to make himself another drink and waves away my apology.

"Nah," he says, "that's what you guys do."

When he comes back in, I ask him if he knows of any enemies his parents might have had.

He shakes his head.

"Like I said, they were everybody's favorite parents, and they had about a million adult friends. I don't think anybody who ran afoul of the bank blamed it on Dad.

"One regret I have is that we can't really do a memorial service until this damn COVID shit is over. They have a cemetery plot up in Staunton, and their funeral would have drawn half the town. Hell of a note for them. It would have been a great sendoff."

He stops for a moment to compose himself.

"But, no, I can't think of anybody who would have wanted to harm them, let alone murder them. And cutting off my father's fingers . . ."

He looks across the room.

"I can't remember anybody speaking ill of them in the last thirty years."

I take note of the time limit and ask about it.

"Ah, hell," he says, "it's ancient history, but there was this trial . . ."

He says he doesn't remember much about it. He was just a kid at the time.

"It had something to do with this couple he knew who were murdered. I think their name was Broom. I just remember that it shook Dad up pretty good, and he was not easily spooked. But that was a long time ago, and, really, nobody was more enemy-free than my parents."

We talk awhile longer. McCaskill says he thinks the couple's daughter was convicted of doing Mom and Dad, and that she got a life sentence. I'm out of there by six thirty, expressing sincere sympathy to a man who looked like he could use some.

On the way back to the paper, I roll it around in my head. Nothing was taken in the McCaskill slayings, which kind of adds to my doubts about Sly Simms doing the deed. If he'd robbed one dead man, why not rob the McCaskills? And if not robbery, then what the fuck was the motive? And what's the story with the fingers?

It isn't making much sense. I don't think the guy in jail did the deed, but I'm damned if I have any idea who did.

CHAPTER NINE

Thursday, January 14

M ARCUS HAS been trying unsuccessfully to get Sly Simms out of jail on bond. I tell him about talking with Kevin McCaskill, and about the strange connection his parents had with Harlan Bell.

"So they both knew about this girl and her parents' murders, what, thirty-three years ago?"

I tell him that she's serving a life sentence, which truly is a life sentence here. Virginia takes a harsh view of parricide.

But Marcus reminds me of something I'd somehow forgotten. The state did not do away with parole until 1995. If this Broom person did the deed eight years before that, she had reason to hope.

"I'm going to check with the department of corrections this morning," I tell Marcus, "but I'd be damned surprised if she's free, if she's even alive."

He wishes me luck.

"This Simms character is a sad case," he tells me. "He's like a child. I'm hoping I can get a shrink to test him. From where I sit, the over/under on his IQ is about seventy."

So I go back into the kitchen nook and have breakfast with my beloved and our cats, which are beloved only by her. Cindy complains that I use too much force evicting Butterball from my chair. I tell her that if Butterball doesn't go on a diet soon, she's going to give me a hernia. The feline replies by hissing at me. Rags, whose ass I saved from life on the streets, offers no support.

I start to tell Cindy about the strange link between our most notorious homicides of late when the phone buzzes on the kitchen table.

It's Peachy.

"Sorry to disturb you, but I knew you'd want to know. There's been another one."

I'm sure I know what she means, but I let her tell me anyhow.

This one was in a neighborhood off Monument a few blocks west of the Downtown Expressway. It's not that far from where Peachy and Ronald live. I jot down the address, thank my old buddy, and promise to pay her back soon for her kindness.

"Pay her back how?" Cindy inquires when I disconnect. She pretty much knows Peachy and I once were friends with benefits, although I've wisely never gone into detail about the benefits.

I assure her that my gratitude will be confined to a free meal or a couple of drinks. I remind her that I am on the far side of my sixtieth birthday, far too feeble to partake in more demonstrative shows of affection.

"So that's all that's stopping you?" she asks.

She observes that I'm underestimating myself. Seeing that anything else I say is liable to be held against me, I take the Fifth, finish my bagel, and leave quietly.

Peachy told me the victim was a doctor of some kind.

I find the house, a two-story brick fortress on a quiet side street. The cops are milling about, mostly being use-less. The chief seems dismayed to see me. As usual, he asks me how I knew about the murder. As usual, I tell him I have my sources.

But then he turns startlingly helpful in giving me some basic facts. Maybe this is L.D.'s way of paying me back a bit for not breaking the story about the mayor running for higher office.

Lemuel Cartwright was a sixty-eight-year-old semiretired psychiatrist until last night, when somebody damn near cut his head off. Yep. A knife, apparently a very large one.

And this one will throw a monkey wrench into Marshall Pitts's campaign against overplaying white victimization.

The late Dr. Cartwright was Black.

They found him in his bed, which was something of a mess. Whoever did the deed must have slipped in sometime after he retired for the evening. The detective who is allowed to speak to me says they figure the guy had been dead for somewhere between six and nine hours.

"What about the fingers?" I ask.

The dick looks over at L.D., who nods his head.

"Yeah," he says, "whoever did it also did a little surgery, after the guy was dead apparently."

"Three fingers?" I guess. "Pinkie, ring, and middle?"

The dick looks a little surprised.

"How the fuck did you know that?"

He apparently hasn't been keeping up with our local maniac's cutlery history.

They don't let me go any farther than the bedroom door, which is barred by crime tape. They've already moved the body, but I can see the bed, whose sheets are more red than white.

"Like a damn abattoir," the chief says.

L.D. is being more helpful than usual this morning. I resist the urge to ask him if he's an alien who's stolen the chief's body.

Of course I'm soon hit with the old quid pro quo.

He pulls me aside.

"Willie," he says, "we really need to keep this shit quiet. I mean, the part about the fingers and all."

Much as I'd like to help my old frenemy, this is a bridge too fucking far.

"L.D., don't you think the population needs to know there's somebody out there butchering people and collecting their fingers?"

His weak-ass argument is that the city will go batshit when they learn that the finger count has gone up, meaning Sly Simms, unless he somehow managed to magically disappear from the lockup for a few hours last night, is almost certainly not a murderer.

"What if it was a copycat?" the chief asks. "What if he read about those other missing fingers and decided to take over the job? Or what if some other lunatic reads this and decides to go for four?"

This is crazy talk, as far as I'm concerned, and I tell L.D. so.

"No matter how scary this is, the public needs to know. I can't sit on this one."

I figure the only reason he let the detective confirm about the fingers was because he knew I'd guessed it already.

I ask the chief if the mayor is still holding fast to Sly Simms as the guilty party.

"I haven't talked to the son of a bitch this morning," L.D. says, "but I'm sure he'll be putting out a statement dumping this steaming mess in my lap."

"Good thing you've got backup," I tell him, referencing his use of Jimbo Stefanski.

"I hope I don't have to use him, but if Mr. Mayor tries to put this one on me and my people, he's in for a shock. And all that, I need not remind you, is off the record."

He swears that the cops are trying to find the woman who tried to abduct little Anna Pratt, but they've turned up nothing.

"And nobody around here saw anything suspicious last night. We've been going door to door. Had to have happened after bedtime. This seems like an early-to-bed neighborhood."

He stops me as I head out to the car to shed the mask long enough for a Camel break.

"You're really going to run with this?"

"Afraid so, L.D. There's no other way."

"Well," he huffs, "just see if you ever get anything from me again."

Yeah, I'm thinking as I head down the brick walkway to my car, next time I'll have to depend on Peachy, as usual.

✦ ✦ ✦

IT TAKES me fifteen minutes to get to the newsroom and another thirty to write the draft that will go online, no doubt with typos and misspellings. Who needs copy editors? Ours are as worthless as a screen door on a submarine.

The TV stations are all over it, of course. One of the teasers: "Dogtown slasher branches out." However none of them have the information provided to me by L.D.'s detective, about the fingers. Gotta give the chief credit for rare cooperation, although he's probably already regretting throwing me that tidbit.

"Jesus, Willie," Sarah says when she reads my online offering, "this shit is getting serious."

By now, people in China probably know that Sylvester Simms is not a mass murderer. He's still locked up, though, so the mayor can save face.

Hizzoner does indeed put out a press release just before one P.M. He seems to be doubling down on Simms, which seems kind of dumb to me, but he's left himself an out.

"If it turns out that our police department has acted too hastily in its honest attempt to find a vicious killer, rest assured that there will be a reckoning."

I'm reckoning that a smart mayor would not try to throw Larry Doby Jones's ample ass under the bus, but maybe "smart" is not in Hizzoner's toolbox.

I do some research on the late Dr. Cartwright. Born in Baltimore, went to the University of Virginia, then UVa medical school.

And then, this:

From 1986 to 1992, he had a practice in Staunton.

I go back and check my notes. It might be a coincidence, but from the late 1980s until sometime in the early '90s, Harlan Bell, the McCaskills, and Dr. Cartwright all lived in or around the same Shenandoah Valley town.

This isn't the kind of confluence that would do much for L.D. Jones, who prefers cold, hard facts to theories. However, romantic bastard that I am, it intrigues me.

I have a couple of hours before my night cops duties begin, and I'm already at the paper, so, what the hell. Might as well make a fourteen-hour day of it. I order chili from the Red Door across the street and then start digging.

I remember Mrs. Bell telling me about the only person she can remember who ever had a grudge against her husband. She gave me the year, 1988, but couldn't remember much else about it. I need to know more about that long-ago trial. It's 1:45 on a Thursday afternoon, I have nothing better to do, and I've got a hunch.

So I call Ella Minopee, a journalist down in Martinsville. She's an old friend and former coworker who drank her way out of Richmond but has landed on her feet. She even helped me nail down an award-worthy story last year. Hell, we both got one of those nifty plastic plaques.

I remember that Ella grew up in Staunton.

When I mention the basics of that trial, Ella lights up.

"Hell, yeah, I remember that," she says, stopping long enough for what sounds like a world-class smoker's cough. Ella and I used to take smoke breaks together. "Maiden fuckin' Broom. What a piece of work."

Ella says she was sixteen when it happened "pretty much the same age as Maiden, so it kind of interested me.

"We didn't know her folks, but everybody knew of the Brooms. That story had everything: Rich eccentrics stabbed to death by their crazy daughter. And the trial was something. Some big-shot lawyer defended her, but there wasn't much doubt that she did it."

Ella promises that she will get me, either electronically or paper, a rundown on the crime and the punishment.

"But why do you want to know about the Broom case?" she asks. "That shit's ancient history."

I explain, trying not to sound overly crazy, about the recent unpleasantness here in Richmond and the Staunton connection, noting that one victim's spouse said the last person she remembered being mad at her husband was the woman I'm now told is named Maiden Broom. Then I told her about the McCaskills and Dr. Cartwright. And about little Anna Pratt and her grandfather.

"Grasping at straws, huh, Willie? Well, you've pulled out a winner before. Go get 'em."

Ella says she's hoping to hang on for a while at the Martinsville paper, but another chain, maybe even cheaper than the Grimm Group, has bought it.

"We might not even be a daily much longer."

She says she's looking into teaching at the local community college.

"The good news," she says, "is that I can't even afford liquor on what they pay down here."

She promises to be back in touch as soon as she's able to get her hands on whatever she can cajole out of her sources back in Staunton.

When I tell Sarah and Wheelie about the Staunton connection, they are less than totally impressed but tell me to keep plugging. On my own time, of course.

Benson Stine, our publisher who is unaffectionately referred to in the newsroom as BS, comes by to see what we're doing to stir up the populace regarding a demented serial killer.

"I see the TV folks are calling him the Dogtown Slasher," he says. "Can't we come up with something catchy? How about the Dogtown Demon?"

We answer noncommittally, because asking your publisher if he's lost his fucking mind is not a good career move.

When he wanders away, Sarah says, "Jesus Christ. What does he think we're doing, naming a sports team? 'How 'bout those Dogtown Demons?'"

✦ ✦ ✦

ABOUT THE time I officially clock in for my night on the police beat, I get a call from Awesome Dude.

He has found Diego.

"He's right skittish," Awesome says, "but he told me he'd talk to you, if I was there to kind of shop around."

I think he means "chaperone."

At any rate, the man in question is now hanging out in Monroe Park, right beneath our little aerie at the Prestwould.

"Be back in fifteen minutes," I tell Sally Velez, who doubts it.

Monroe Park has had a makeover. They've offended the tree-huggers by cutting down a bunch of hardwoods.

They've replaced the cracked asphalt that used to criss-cross it with paths more suitable to a park. It's well-lighted and has lots of inducements for the college kids. It's also less enticing to Richmond's homeless population, which maybe was the idea in the first place.

All the prettification hasn't kept Diego away, at least not today.

I meet Awesome there, and he leads me to Diego.

The guy's a mess. He's wearing somebody's hand-me-down overcoat with a couple of buttons missing, what appear to be two pairs of work pants, and a politically incorrect Washington Redskins toboggan. He appears to be from somewhere south of the border and, like Awesome, is only moderately conversant in English. There's something wrong with his eyes, in that they do not seem to be attached to each other and wander off in different directions.

It occurs to me that he is not anybody's idea of a reliable witness to anything, including his name. I'm also thinking that the last thing Diego would want to do is be in the crosshairs of the authorities, especially those concerned with immigration.

He does seem to have a decent memory though.

"Yes," he says after Awesome, interpreting his broken English, asks him to describe his interactions with Sylvester Simms back on the seventh. "That is right. We was together that night, me and Sly, out of the cold in some rich man's garage. He don't kill nobody, not that night."

Diego gives enough detail, including the kind of cheap-ass wine the two of them were sharing, and even describes where the garage is.

"But don't tell nobody, because we might need it again."

They had managed to get locked out of the homeless shelter nearby on that cold evening, and Diego makes it clear that he needs to get his ass over there soon so that doesn't happen again tonight.

I give the guy ten bucks. Maybe he can buy another layer of clothing, unless he gets thirsty first.

He says "*Muchas gracias*," and then he's gone.

I thank Awesome for his trouble and then drive over three blocks west of the park and find the garage exactly the way Diego described it. There are no lights on in the attached townhouse. I figure the joint belongs to snowbirds working on their tans down in Florida. When they get back, maybe they'll wonder who their mystery guests were. They might even report it to the cops, if they've got time to waste.

I call Marcus and tell him about my interview with Diego.

"And you didn't hang on to him, at least find out where we could get up with him?"

"Marcus, trust me. You do not want this guy on any witness stand. I'm just telling you so we both know damn sure that Sylvester Simms didn't kill anybody. This Diego is impaired and he's probably illegal."

"Well," he says, "it still would have been good to talk to him."

I explain that I've already talked to him, and I can vouch for everything I just said.

He harrumphs and hangs up.

There isn't much sense in even telling the chief about this. L.D. doesn't really want to know about any undocumented residents in his city. He and I see hounding them as a waste of precious police time and a little bit like afflicting the afflicted.

With four murders now on the books, including one when Sly Simms was in the pokey, the testimony of one poor, lost Mexican shouldn't even be necessary to show that mistakes have been made.

"Shouldn't" is the operative word.

✦ ✦ ✦

BACK AT the paper, we're already feeling the effects of a full-blown shit-yourself panic, even before my print-edition story and sidebar on the latest killing hits the sidewalks tomorrow morning. Chuck Apple checks with the local gun shops, where business is, as he wincingly wrote in his lede, "going great guns." In Richmond, we might be up to two weapons per adult by now, one for each hand.

As if that weren't enough, it comes on top of all the COVID crap. We've now gone from hoping for a vaccine to knowing that it's out there and we can't get it.

Some of us have gone from vaccine deniers to vaccine addicts, looking for a fix wherever we can find it. They're only supposed to be sticking the old and infirm, but there are, as always, those who think they are entitled by birthright to a place at the front of the line. Callie Ann Boatwright came across a beaut today as she called around to local hospitals and clinics on the vaccine situation. A bunch of house peddlers almost managed to finesse their fat asses into the line at a local pharmacy. When Callie Ann, told of the plot, called up the head realtor, he hemmed and hawed for a while, trying to brazen it out.

Then he hung up, but he called back five minutes later and said he and his gang had decided to forgo the opportunity "in order to ensure that those precious shots go to those who need them more."

"He made it sound like he was doing it as a favor," Callie Ann told me. "And then he begged me not to write anything about it, since they decided to back off."

I observed that this was like robbers, fleeing a bank empty-handed because the cops showed up, claiming "no harm, no foul."

"Exactly," Callie Ann said. "He said it would paint an unfair picture of a group that does a lot of good for the community. I told him I'd think about it."

Surely, I said, you aren't going to sit on this one.

She laughed.

"Fat fucking chance."

Hanging around a newsroom has done great damage to Callie Ann's innocence and vocabulary, I fear.

There isn't much else to do about Sylvester Simms's plight and the interrelated puzzle of who the hell actually did kill four of our residents. I'm putting great store, though, in Ella Minopee's doggedness, hoping she can help me shed some light on a long-ago crime 100 miles away.

Cindy is waiting up when I get home not long after midnight.

When we're in bed and I tell her about Diego, she is mostly concerned about the man himself.

"And you just left him like that, without getting an address or anything?"

"He doesn't have any address, and I gave him ten bucks."

"Big spender," my beloved says. "Well, I'm going to keep an eye out for him in the park. I mean, it could have been Abe out there."

OK, I salvaged Abe Custalow all those years ago when I found him residing in Monroe Park, but Abe was my best friend growing up. He'd had my back a hundred times.

"You can't save everybody," I say.

"You can try," is her response. She looks over where Butterball and the recently salvaged Rags are curled up next to each other in the corner.

"Maybe," I suggest, "we could give Diego a cat."

Cindy's sense of humor comes and goes. At this moment, it's gone.

CHAPTER TEN

Friday, January 15

I GET a call at home before nine from a man I know who lives out at Brandermill, a community about eighteen miles and a hundred light-years from Richmond. It's an instant middle- and upper-middle-class community where crime hardly ever rears its ugly head.

The guy out at Brandermill is a cop. Getting a tip from a cop is a rarity for your hardworking police reporter, but Art Smallwood isn't part of the city force anymore, opting for better hours and fewer dirt naps as part of the Chesterfield County police. As such, I guess he feels less constrained about sharing.

Plus, I did once save him a bit of embarrassment, if not worse, by not writing what I knew for a change. What I knew was that Mr. Smallwood pulled a Barney Fife, accidentally shooting himself in the foot while giving chase to a young felon in Creighton Court. I heard about it through an old Oregon Hill fuck buddy who was then a nurse at the hospital where the self-inflicted victim turned up.

When I confronted Smallwood, he begged me not to write about it. It was an inconsequential wound. Only he and his partner knew, and his partner promised not to tell.

So I didn't tell either. It didn't seem to matter that much, and it might have ended the guy's career. Two years later, he left the city force anyhow for the joys of Chesterfield.

This morning, the bread I cast upon the waters came back as a tasty seven-layer cake.

Smallwood told me what happened. Unlike his boo-boo a few years ago, this one will be on the news eventually whether I write it or not.

"I just thought you might want to have a heads-up," he said.

What happened was that a Brandermillian came home late from an alleged poker night and thought he could sneak in quietly, without waking his wife, who might wonder where the fuck he'd been until two in the morning.

Trouble was, he did wake her. Further trouble was that he'd bought her a neat little pistol last week, just after our serial killer started getting famous. He gave her a rudimentary lesson in how to use it.

She used it well enough. Not realizing that Hubby wasn't sleeping next to her on their king-size bed, she assumed the footsteps she heard were those of a demented, knife-wielding psychopath.

Before she realized the error of her ways, she'd plugged her husband three times.

"He said that, if I felt threatened, to just keep firing," she told the Chesterfield police. "So I did."

She got him once in the shoulder and twice in the right arm. He'll live, but I'm thinking he might want to give his beloved a Louisville slugger to replace that pistol.

It's not that difficult to get in touch with the county cops' media person and get confirmation, since I have most of the facts already. When I called them, neither the husband nor the wife was at all interested in talking about their little adventure. Hell, who would be? But, unlike Smallwood's little screwup, this one's going to be out there anyhow. Smallwood said that one of the local TV stations had already called. I might as well post it online before the good-hair people put it on the air.

I check my email. Nothing yet from Ella.

Cindy's off for a teachers' meeting. So, with time to kill, I drop by Oregon Hill to see Peggy. She and Awesome are watching some mindless morning talk show, engulfed in a marijuana fog that no doubt makes it more entertaining. Though they seem to have no lingering problems since their bout with COVID, I worry about some of the long-term effects.

"Long term?" my old mom asks. "Why the hell do I have to worry about long-term effects? Long term isn't exactly on my list of concerns."

She might have a point. She is seventy-eight. I mention, though, being a good son, that I hope she makes it to 100.

She snorts.

"I hope to hell not. Seventy-eight is hard enough."

She tells me, though, that Andi has some news.

"You can't pass it on?"

"Nah, she wanted to tell you herself. She just came by last night and said she'd get in touch with you today."

"Good news or bad news?" I ask.

Peggy smiles.

"You'll have to ask her yourself."

So I call my daughter from Peggy's living room.

She's home when she answers. She's working virtually these days like just about everybody else. Since William, my grandson, is getting his schooling via Zoom, they're spending a lot of time together.

"What's up?" I ask.

"I wanted to tell you in person," she says, "but I guess this'll do. William, tell your granddad the big news."

She hands the phone to William.

"I'm gonna be a big brother," he says.

Yes, after "trying" for a couple of years, Andi and Walter are pregnant. Actually I imagine only Andi is pregnant.

I congratulate William and his mother on the big news. My happiness is pretty much complete. As a grandparent, more grandkids are an unalloyed blessing. You get to spoil them, and when you get tired of them, you send them home to their parents. Having been an only child, I always envied my friends their big, bustling families.

Plus I have faith in the innate goodness of Walter McGinnis. My son-in-law is not exactly Mr. Excitement, but I believe he'll always treat young William as his own, no matter how many babies he and my daughter make.

I congratulate Andi, also, on her unerring good judgment, which she must have gotten from her mother. She could have married the relentlessly worthless Thomas Jefferson Blandford V, William's biological father, out of desperation or need. But she peered into Quip's empty soul and knew there were worse things than being a single mom. She held out for something better, which turned out to be Walter.

Before I go, I ask her, "You don't have a gun, do you?" I relate the Brandermill story to her.

"Good Lord, no," she says. "Walter bought me a baseball bat."

After more congratulations and general bonhomie, I ring off, my day made already.

✦ ✦ ✦

WHEN I check my email again, Ella Minopee has come through.

She has sent me a message complete with five attachments. All of them, she informs me, are stories that pretty much sum up the sad demise of Beverley and Constance Broom and the events that followed.

I've already gone to the electronic archives and read what my paper wrote about that long-ago incident, but I was sure the paper in Staunton would have covered it like the Second Coming. I was right.

I grab a sandwich from Perly's and head for the newsroom. I'll want to put something more substantial together on the Brandermill clusterfuck and do what follow-up I can cobble together on what is now the upper-case Dogtown Slasher story. And it'll be easier to check out everything Ella's sent me if I use my work computer.

I'm barely off the elevator when I see a crowd gathered around Sally Velez's terminal. Chuck Apple, Leighton Byrd, and a couple of photographers all seem to be having a wonderful time.

"You're not going to believe this," Sally says as I join the crowd.

I've often heard the expression, "screwed the pooch," and found it to be a little illogical, having never known anyone to admit to really having had sex with a canine. However, our Weather Guy has given the phrase a whole new meaning.

Weather Guy, Guy Flowers, has apparently screwed the pooch because his pooch screwed another pooch.

It's all on video. Weather Guy uses the paper's website to post little weather chats every day, inspired by the on-air shenanigans of the TV stations' meteorologists. To add to the "awww" element, he has been making good use of those Labrador retrievers he "borrowed."

"The idiot said he didn't know one of them was a girl," Bootie Carmichael informs me as they start to play the clip again.

"He knows now," Chuck Apple says.

"So does half of Richmond," adds Leighton.

I never saw his earlier videos, but apparently Weather Guy's act played well the first four times, with the pups

playfully rolling around in the grass and licking themselves in the background while WG told us how cold it
was outside.

The fifth time, done this morning, was not a charm.

"Damn," Leighton says as the action in the background
becomes more interesting than anything he's saying.
"That's pretty intense."

"Are you old enough to watch this?" I ask.

Weather Guy has to stop his meteorological monologue
to encourage his new pets to get a room, but they don't
seem so inclined. The male, as a matter of fact, appears to
try to bite him before the video goes dark.

"Why did they do it live?" I ask.

"You can be damn sure they won't be doing it live
again," Sally says.

Our readers/viewers who saw the performance are
mostly amused, it seems. By the time I've watched the
doggie porn episode, just before the site was temporarily shut down, Apple has checked the online comments.
Although a few in our audience allege to be appalled,
most of the thirty-two who have weighed in already find it
highly entertaining.

Sarah Goodnight has wandered over. As a full-fledged
newsroom manager, she is not allowed to be amused.

"Damn," she says, "I hope BS doesn't see the comments. He'll want to make the dogs a regular feature."

"Give the readers what they want," I advise.

✦ ✦ ✦

I BANG out a few inches on the shooting in Brandermill and
then do a follow on the latest serial killing, with little else
to report. The deceased shrink apparently didn't have a
wife or kids, and his parents are dead. The three missing

fingers, bringing the total of purloined digits to six, add a little gruesome intrigue to the story.

By two thirty, I'm ready to tuck into whatever Ella Minopee sent me.

✦ ✦ ✦

THE DEED was done on Halloween 1987. The Brooms didn't show up at the country club for dinner with friends the next night. One of those friends went knocking when they didn't answer their phone, and he's the one who saw a body through a bedroom window and called the sheriff's department.

It was, according to the newspaper report, a mess. In the foyer and bedroom where the killings took place, the bed and the floors were blood-soaked. It spattered on the walls.

"I never seen anything like it," was the quote from one deputy.

The first report notes that the Brooms had a daughter, Maiden, who was sixteen, and a son, Beverley Jr., known as Buddy, seventeen. Neither one of them reportedly was present at the time of the murders but had not yet been located.

Reading this, I'm amazed that any law enforcement entity was so free with information. L.D. would have sat on this for three days if he could have gotten away with it.

The next attachment is a story that ran two days later. That's how long it took for the authorities to find Maiden. The brother, it was noted, had still not been located.

The article includes a photo of Maiden, taken from a private-school yearbook of a school that hadn't kicked her ass out yet. She looks, in the picture, like a normal, carefree teenage girl, although her smile looks almost like a smirk.

They found her at a motel in Virginia Beach. She said she had gone to the beach to meet some friends, but she couldn't remember their names. As for her brother, she had no idea where he might be.

She appeared to be suitably shocked to discover that she was now an orphan, but already a careful reader could see that the story wasn't exactly holding together. There was, for instance, evidence of dried blood on the seat of the family Buick she had borrowed, and Maiden didn't appear to have any overnight clothing with her.

The next attachment was from ten days later and was a stem-winder catching readers up on everything that had happened so far.

In the interim, the sheriff's department had found the murder weapon, a big-ass knife with dried blood on it, in the woods alongside the road leading into the Brooms' substantial property. It appeared, the sheriff said, that someone had thrown it out a car window. And, yes, it was the Brooms' blood. But they couldn't get a decent print off the knife.

Fingerprints in the bedroom and foyer did match those of Maiden Broom, but, as she pointed out, she lived there. Of course her fingerprints were everywhere. The other prints were assumed to belong to her missing brother.

A friend of Maiden's surfaced in the meantime. The girl's mother told the cops that Maiden and Buddy had come by the afternoon before and had gone to a Halloween party with their daughter. The daughter claimed at first that the siblings had stayed the night, she and Maiden sharing the double bed and Buddy sleeping on the couch in her bedroom, which had a separate entrance.

It didn't take long for her story to fall apart, though, and she finally admitted that the Brooms had left the house at six thirty the night before and had not gone to the party with her.

There still was no sign of Buddy, and Maiden continued to claim, along with her innocence, that she had no idea where her brother was.

Maiden Broom was charged with capital murder. Her father's safe had been ransacked, and Maiden paid cash for the motel room, so conclusions were drawn.

I would have been covering the state legislature when all this happened, covering our state representatives' moral misdemeanors. A double homi in the Shenandoah Valley didn't really register with me at the time.

Maiden Broom had a lawyer, and the lawyer told the paper that the whole affair was a "cruel miscarriage of justice," and that his client would be proved innocent, a girl recently orphaned who was suffering the mental torture of being accused of their murders.

The fourth installment was from six months later. That's how long it took for the case to come to trial. It was filed the day the verdict was announced. The headline, in seventy-two-point type, simply screamed GUILTY.

The trial had lasted four days. There were witnesses to Maiden Broom's basic goodness, but there were a lot of dissenting voices.

And that's when the pieces started falling into place.

There was a young Harlan Bell, testifying that he had been witness to violent arguments between the victims and their daughter while he was doing some plumbing work at the Broom mansion.

"She said she was going to kill them," Bell was quoted as saying.

When asked by the defense counsel if maybe that wasn't just a temper tantrum by a normal sixteen-year-old, Bell said, "That girl isn't any normal sixteen-year-old." The story even noted that the defendant screamed insults at Mr. Bell and spit on him as he was leaving the courtroom.

And then there was Jack McCaskill, who told a couple of similar stories about Maiden Broom's temper. The girl's father told McCaskill that she had set fire to her bed and climbed out the window after she had been grounded. McCaskill also said he witnessed Maiden losing her temper in spectacular fashion while he and Sheila were there playing bridge with her parents.

"She wanted some money to go shopping, and Beverley told her no. He told her two or three times, and she just kind of lost it. She said she'd see them in hell. They just didn't know what to do with her. She'd already been kicked out of a couple of schools."

Jack McCaskill said that the Brooms confided to him and his wife that they were afraid she would do something really awful, but they didn't want to have her committed. They said Maiden was very clever about hiding her true nature whenever she was force-marched to a counselor.

When McCaskill left the stand, Maiden tried to spit on him, too, but, according to the article, she didn't have the range.

The last story was written three months later, after the sentencing. It told the whole sorry story all over again, with a few more details.

I had forgotten about Wilson Pratt, Anna's grandfather, and the earlier stories didn't mention the commonwealth's attorney. But there he was, commenting on his pleasure over justice being served. He said he would not have been unhappy to see sixteen-year-old Maiden Broom sent to the gas chamber, but the judge took her age into account, and they settled for life in prison.

There was also more detail about the trial. Before it went to court, the state brought in a shrink who was supposed to make a judgment as to whether Maiden was insane enough to send her to one of our fine mental institutions.

The young psychiatrist assigned to interview her said that she did not rise to the state's standard, effectively throwing Maiden on the mercy of the criminal justice system.

It might have been Lemuel Cartwright's first job after his residency.

My head is spinning. I walk to the coffee room for a cup, trying to sort it out.

When I get back to my desk, I walk over to Sara's office and tell her what I've learned.

She's just gotten off the phone with one of our readers who felt that a video of dogs screwing was not in the best of taste.

"Weather Guy said the friend he borrowed them from was going to have the female fixed. I told him I'd have him fixed if he ever showed up on camera again with a canine of any type.

"That's beyond crazy," she agrees when I tell her what I learned about that long-ago crime. She suggests that it would be a good idea to check with the state criminal justice folks and find out if Maiden Broom is still a ward of the state.

"She ought to be," she says. "I mean, even if she did it before they abolished parole, there's no way she's out, running free. Is there?"

"Shouldn't be, but from what I just read, it might be a good idea to make sure."

Then I call L.D. Jones at police headquarters. He's left for the day, his aide informs me.

I'm under orders to never buzz the chief on his cell phone unless there is a real or imminent shitstorm.

I'm thinking it might be time to break out the umbrellas.

I catch him in his car on the way home.

"This had better be important," he says when he picks up. "You're causing me to break city law by talking on my cell phone while driving."

I tell him that if he gets pulled, he can probably get the ticket fixed.

Then I tell him he might want to pull over.

When I've told him what I know and suspect, I hear him sigh.

"Is there anything you do that doesn't cause me trouble?"

He says that the mayor is digging in his heels on releasing Sylvester Simms.

"He says it will look like we don't know what the fuck we're doing. Maybe this will change his mind."

Meanwhile he says he will check with the parole board "but those people are pretty stingy with information. Not very helpful."

"Physician, heal thyself," I advise.

He advises something profane.

"One thing," L.D. says. "They have to inform the family of the victims if they're considering parole."

I tell him I'll see if I can find a living relative of the Brooms. The only ones I know about are either supposed to be in prison for murdering them or disappeared after that fateful event.

I call Ella in Martinsville to thank her for her help and to ask if she knows of any living relatives of the Brooms who might have been informed of parole hearings.

She says she'll call her sister in Staunton.

She calls back in half an hour.

"Nobody's seen hide nor hair of Beverley Junior since that day," she says, "but Beverley Senior does have a younger brother who's still around. He lives up in the valley. I'm guessing he's close to eighty by now. I have his phone number and his address."

I tell Ella what a prize she is and ask her not to mention this to anyone until I've nailed it down.

She tells me Weather Guy's dog show has gone viral.

"I saw it on the news in Roanoke," she says. "They had to, you know, kind of pixilate it, but it was still entertaining."

I tell her that we live to entertain.

Sarah's door is open, so I invite myself in.

"We need to run with this," I tell her.

"Does anybody else know about the connection?"

"Not that I know of."

I tell her that I'm sure Ella won't spill the beans.

"Then why don't you wait a day and see if you can find out anything from the brother? We really need to make sure that this Maiden Broom is still locked up, although it does make you wonder."

It does indeed. Four people are dead who all either pissed off Maiden Broom almost thirty-four years ago or were married to someone who did. Plus the attack on the granddaughter of the commonwealth's attorney.

I reluctantly agree that I won't write the story until I've gotten in touch with Beverley Broom Senior's brother. Sitting on news for a day makes my butt itch. I'm not likely, though, to get beaten on this one.

If Maiden's still where she should be, we've got the strangest set of coincidences imaginable. If not, we've got something even weirder than that.

I try the brother's number three times. Each time someone picks up on the other end and then hangs up before I can say anything. If Mr. Broom is like me, he assumes anyone calling him from an unknown number is somebody in Slovenia trying to separate him from his money.

Well, I know he's home. It's a little more than two hours to Staunton from here. Maybe it'll be a slow night and I will have the energy to drive up there tomorrow.

CHAPTER ELEVEN

Saturday, January 16

CARSON BROOM lives just west of Staunton, on a gravel road off the US highway, in postcard country halfway between the Blue Ridge and the Alleghenies. With more sleep, I probably could have enjoyed the great outdoors a little more. At least I had company. Cindy even offered to drive up so I could stack a few z's.

As often happens when I wish for a slow night, last evening was a three-ring circus. Two homis a couple of streets apart on the North Side occupied me until after midnight. By the time I'd filed for our website and finally crawled into bed, it was damn near two A.M.

We manage to get away by nine, though, and we find the sign leading to the Broom estate by eleven fifteen.

I don't know if the guy will even talk to me, but I don't know what else to do at this point.

"Holy crap," Cindy says as we make our way up the half-mile road and see chez Broom for the first time. "It looks like a damn castle."

It kind of does. It's three stories, counting the attic, all red brick and as deep as it is wide. There's a huge expanse of land around it.

"Must be five thousand square feet at least," she reckons.

On closer inspection, the place could use some work. The paint's peeling pretty badly around the windows and it needs a new roof. Crabgrass is growing between the cracks in the brick walkway. It looks like a house that's grown old with its owner. And the land seems like nobody's using it for anything except growing a good crop of weeds.

We are in luck though. After pressing the doorbell a couple of times and deducing that it doesn't work, I try knocking. In half a minute or so, I hear shuffling, and half a minute after that, the door opens.

"What do you want?" the man asks. He's definitely at least eighty. He's using a cane, and he squints as if he can't quite make us out. And, of course, he's holding a gun. "If you're selling anything, you need to get the hell out and quit bothering me."

He confirms that he is, indeed, Carson Broom. I explain, as quickly as I can, who I am and why we've come. He does, to my relief, put down his weapon.

"No, hell no," he says when I ask if he knows if his niece has been paroled. "Last time that little bitch was up for parole, I drove all the way to Richmond to make sure it didn't happen."

I ask him when that was.

He says it was last May.

"The parole board wrote later and said she wouldn't have another shot at it in five years, and I'll be there then, too, God willing."

He lets us come inside, where things are worse than on the exterior. There are cats, and someone hasn't been doing a good job of maintaining the litter boxes. For once, I'm thankful for the mask.

Carson Broom looks around.

"This was their place," he says.

When the Brooms were murdered, and their daughter was arrested and convicted, and their son disappeared, Carson became the nominal owner.

"If Buddy ever shows up, I guess it's his, but he's gone. Hell, she probably killed him, too, and they never found his body."

Carson moved into the place after his wife died.

"I've tried to keep it up, but it's gettin' to be too damn much."

He even shows me the bedroom where his brother and sister-in-law were killed.

"If you look close," he says, "you can still see stains on the floor."

We leave Cat City as soon as I can semi-gracefully manage it. Mr. Broom walks us to the front door, almost tripping on a couple of tabbies that seem intent on being the death of their meal ticket.

On the way back to Richmond, we wonder aloud why anyone would move into a place with that kind of misery attached to it. I don't believe in ghosts, but even I would be afraid to spend the night in that joint.

"If anything ever happens to me," I tell Cindy as we're enjoying an unhealthy lunch at a great fried chicken place along the highway, "please tell me you won't turn into the cat lady."

"That poor man," she says. "Those cats probably turned up there as strays, and he just couldn't say no."

"Like I said."

"Don't worry, Willie. I think Kate probably would draw the line at two cats anyhow."

Zero would have been a better number, I'm thinking.

✦ ✦ ✦

Now we know that the parole board scotched Maiden Broom's last effort at parole.

To make double damn sure that she's still a ward of the state, though, I need to check.

I phone Leighton Byrd as Cindy drives over Afton Mountain. In our paper's straitened circumstances, reporters have to wear more than one hat, and among Leighton's chapeaux is the one that makes her the go-to person for the state prison system. She's a quick study fortunately.

She knows what I'm working on, and she's more than eager, at two on a Saturday afternoon, to check around. Leighton smells double byline. Fine with me. It's worth giving up a little credit to nail this down.

"You might have to wait until Monday," I tell her.

She tells me that she has an in with the flack who doles out information on who and where the inmates are, and he might be willing to tell her what she needs to know this afternoon.

"He's kind of cute," she says. Leighton has her ways.

I drop Cindy off at the Prestwould just in time to make it to work only twenty minutes late.

I tell Sarah what I learned in Staunton.

"And the guy lives in the house where they were murdered?" she asks, adding an "Ewww."

Nothing to do after that except wait for crime to erupt and hope I get some information from Leighton.

About four thirty, things get interesting.

I get a call from Andy Peroni. My old buddy never phones me at work. This time, he's got a reason.

"You know that girl that was attacked over in Windsor Farms?" he asks. "Well, I think the woman that did it is still out there."

No doubt, I reply.

He explains that he and a friend of his were over at a place on West Main last night. It's the kind of joint that sells more booze than food because the booze is better. It's still open, although COVID law forbids anyone from actually sitting at the bar.

His friend was making the acquaintance of a woman who looked to be in her late forties maybe. When she left, he followed her out to her car.

"And that's when it got weird."

The friend came back inside "looking like he'd seen a ghost." He told Andy that he had tried to make a move on the woman. She opened her car door and slid inside.

"She asked him if he'd like to go for a ride, and he said, 'Sure.' She unlocked the passenger door. Then, when he started to get in, he saw that she was holding this big-ass knife. He said she asked him if he wanted some of that. He said he got the hell out of there."

Andy said the guy was not willing to talk about it.

"Why?"

"Why the fuck do you think? Wedding ring."

I ask him what the woman looked like.

"You must have gotten a pretty good look at her."

"Yeah. Tell you the truth, I was thinking about hitting on her myself."

"Wouldn't Grace be a little put out by that?"

"Hey," Andy says, "I'm trying to give you a hot tip here."

He says the mystery woman was maybe five foot eight, kind of thin, with red hair.

"Thing about the hair though. I'm pretty sure she was wearing a wig."

He says the thing that he remembered most was her eyes.

"She had this look, like she didn't blink but about once a minute. She looked intense, like maybe she was ready for just about anything."

Anything, apparently, except Andy's tomcatting buddy.

I concede that it could have been the same woman who tried to hurt Anna Pratt.

"But you're not going to put any of this in the paper," Andy says.

"How the fuck can I? You haven't given me a name. You haven't reported it to the cops."

I thank him anyhow. It does give me something to chew on.

If Maiden Broom is safely locked away, who's the mystery woman with the knife?

I check in with Peachy at home. I can hear the soon-to-be adopted Aurora squealing in the background. I ask Peachy how instant motherhood is treating her so far.

"It has its moments," she says. "A nanny would be nice, maybe one of them au pairs everybody's getting. But Aurora seems happy as a clam."

"Happy" is a blessed state for a child who was only a few months old when her parents were murdered twenty feet from her crib.

Peachy says the police haven't had any luck finding the woman who attacked the Pratt girl.

I tell her that they might want to direct their attention in the direction of a certain dive on West Main. I explain.

"But you can't give me his name or anything?"

"I don't even know his name," I tell her. I lie and say it was an anonymous call.

"Probably some guy two-timing his wife, but he wanted somebody to know."

I give her the guy's description of his would-be assailant.

"I'll pass it on," she says, "for what good it'll do."

"You all still think you've got the right guy locked up, even after that shrink was murdered?"

"Don't say 'you all' like we're all lock-step. But I know the mayor is digging his heels in. He hates to be wrong."

I note that half the city's out buying guns because they're sure the right suspect is not in the city jail.

She sighs.

"We'll just have to see what happens."

I tell her that, if Maiden Broom's uncle is right, we can be pretty sure that, whoever is wreaking havoc on our fair city, it isn't her.

Then I heard her yell, "Aurora! No! Put that down! Excuse me, Willie. Motherhood calls."

✦ ✦ ✦

SHORTLY AFTER seven, as I'm doing the Sudoku and waiting for Saturday night to break out in the Holy City, Leighton comes over.

"Something's screwy here," she says.

What's screwy is Maiden Broom's current status. Leighton's source with the parole board says they can't comment on whether Ms. Broom is or isn't currently in the hands of the state.

"She's supposed to be at the Virginia Correction Center for Women. I think it's out in Goochland County somewhere."

Yeah, I'm familiar with the place. Once, years ago, I did an interview with a woman who was incarcerated there. She'd been convicted of killing her rich boyfriend, who might possibly have deserved killing. She maintained her innocence while making it clear that the guy had it coming, whoever did it.

She was looking for an advocate. I passed on the opportunity.

It struck me at the time how Virginia has squandered the James River. Over the decades and centuries, we've planted all kinds of lockups along its banks. For a long time, we even had the main state prison, the one where they toasted your ass if it needed toasting, right on the James here in Richmond, just down from Oregon Hill, some of whose natives were usually among its inmates.

If that isn't enough, there are railroad tracks all along the river on one side or the other. Didn't anybody think riverfront property might have been better used for something other than trains and prisons?

Leighton knows that the place in Goochland is where Maiden Broom is supposed to be.

"But my guy can't confirm that she is."

"What the fuck? Is she on vacation? Did they give her a sabbatical?"

"I don't know, Willie. This guy, who's usually pretty loose-lipped, says he can't talk about it."

I tell Leighton what I learned today from Carson Broom.

"Well, damn," she says. "Why didn't you tell me that before? I'm still learning this beat, but I know that ain't right. I mean, if he's the family contact, they've got to let him know if they parole her."

She gets up, somewhat nettled.

"I'm going to call his ass back," she says, "and I'd better get a straight answer this time. Anything else you forgot to tell me, before I jerk this guy's chain?"

I apologize for not mentioning Carson Broom before.

To make up a little for that, I tell Leighton what Andy Peroni told me this afternoon.

"She had a knife, and acted like she wanted to use it?"

"She asked him if he wanted a piece of that, is the way Andy explained it."

"Well, you need to write something about that."

I explain the circumstances.

"Oh, so this guy's lookin' for a little strange, and now you guys are covering for each other. I see."

I try to explain that Andy wouldn't even give me the would-be assaultee's name, and that he told me about it off the record.

"Well," she says, "I hope that whoever this maniac is, he or she doesn't kill somebody else while you're sitting on that little factoid."

If you can get somebody, not for attribution, to say that Maiden Broom is not incarcerated where she's supposed to be incarcerated, I tell her, I can run with that and work in a graf or three about the incident with Andy's friend.

I'm toying with the idea of doing something just this side of hinky. If I write that an anonymous source said a woman fitting a certain description brandished a large knife, apparently similar to the one the cops believe dispatched Harlan Bell, the McCaskills and Dr. Cartwright, outside a Main Street joint on Friday night, and that a woman with a reason to have a grudge against all of them was not locked up where she was supposed to be, that might fit into the scenario I'm damn close to putting in print.

I'm one confirmation away from telling our readers why a double homicide and subsequent trial thirty-three years ago might be connected to our present spate of slashings, and that the cops could well have the wrong sucker locked up.

"Huh," Leighton says, "that would sell some damn papers."

She turns as she's walking away.

"Double byline, right?"

I hesitate, then nod.

Sharing's not my default mode, but if Leighton can provide the missing link, I'm willing to share.

I call Andy, who's at dinner with his wife.

His end of the conversation is a little terse. When I tell him how I might be printing the tidbit he imparted earlier, without naming the source, he just says, "Be damn sure you don't." In the background, I hear Grace ask, "What was that about?"

Before he can go into the hummina-hummina, the phone goes dead.

I'm sure my old pal can come up with something creative to pacify his wife. He's had a lot of practice.

✦ ✦ ✦

I WALK over to Sarah Goodnight's office to tell her what I might be writing.

"That's a lot of maybes," she observes. "And we're going to pay hell getting it into the paper, even if you find out for sure that the Broom woman is on the loose."

I tell my former mentee that I'll do the best I can.

I start writing what I think I know, on the off chance that Leighton's feminine wiles will unearth the last piece of the puzzle from the parole board flack.

There will be time later to flesh it out with actual facts.

It's almost nine thirty when Leighton comes over, a little breathless and her cat's eyes shining.

"Got it," she says.

What's she's got is the deep, dark truth that Maiden Broom, convicted murderess serving a life sentence, has been paroled.

"My source said he wasn't even sure himself until he checked with some midlevel official he knows. He said everybody had been under strict instructions not to answer any questions about parole, so he figured something was up, but like the good flack he is, he was keeping his head down.

"The guy wouldn't confirm it officially, but he gave me the name and number of the official who confirmed it to him.

"If the shit hits the fan, he doesn't want to have to lie under oath about any of this. He said the woman who confirmed it to him was pretty pissed about the whole thing, and that it went a lot deeper than just Maiden Broom."

So Leighton called the woman.

"And she told me everything, not for attribution, of course, but I think we can run with it."

"You 'think' we can run with it."

"OK, dammit. I'm sure we can run with it. The woman was very specific. She even named a few more names of people who have been paroled without family members getting any notice."

I congratulate Leighton on a job well done.

"My name goes first, right?" she says.

"What?"

"On the double byline."

I want to tell our eager young scribe that maybe she ought to concentrate more on the process than the reward, but she's done a great job, so I just advise her not to press her luck.

I tell Sarah to see if we can hold up for maybe fifteen minutes on locking up and convince her that we're not leading the paper down the primrose path.

"Ten minutes," she says at last. "And I mean ten, not eleven."

I flesh out the story in about half an hour, with Leighton hovering over my shoulder and filling in the blanks. Handley Pace, who's designing A1, has to do some fancy dancing, too, moving a thumb-sucker on the legislature inside, killing one of the warm and fuzzy stories we've poached from another Grimm Group paper to make room for it, and finding photos of the McCaskills to go on the front.

It all comes together with a full minute to spare. Technology is not my bosom buddy, but getting all this to work would have taken a hell of a lot longer back in the Dark Ages when low-paid composing-room folks had to cut and paste everything on the page before it went to press.

Sarah has called Wheelie at home to let him know what we're doing. She says he was somewhat concerned about an unattributed story accusing the state parole board of violating policy and maybe unleashing a mass murderer on the general citizenry. He reminded her of our corporate masters' strong aversion to lawsuits.

"But when I told him what the downside was, holding back information that could alert our readers to the fact that there is almost definitely a psycho loose out there, he finally caved."

Of course, the insomniacs who check out our website in the middle of the night will know all this before the sun comes up. When it all hits the fan, I'm thinking Sunday is not going to be a day of rest. It'll be another good day to own a gun shop.

Sarah takes time to congratulate Handley and Leighton on a job well done. She calls the press foreman to thank him for his forbearance in letting news get in the way of his production schedule. In normal, non-COVID times, she probably would have taken Handley and Leighton both over to Penny Lane for a drink or three.

"How about me?" I ask.

"Yeah," she says, "you didn't do too bad either."

"Hey," Leighton says as she checks out the story online, "they put Willie's byline first."

Alphabetical order, I explain.

CHAPTER TWELVE

Sunday, January 17

THE HEADLINE stretches across the top of A1:

Is paroled killer Dogtown Slasher?

There wasn't time to get the chief's input last night, but he has plenty of it today. I should have shut down my cell phone.

"Why the fuck didn't you call me?" he asks.

I try to explain, but L.D. wants this to be a monologue, not a dialogue.

He rants on about how bad this makes him look, and about how the mayor is already on his ass. Apparently Hizzoner is one of our insomniac online readers.

Finally I'm able to cut in.

"The same mayor who insisted that you had the right guy all along locked up in the city jail?"

"Well, he's not going to be downhill when the shit starts flowing, if he can help it."

I remind him of what he already knows. He's got an ear witness to the mayor's complicity in keeping Simms locked up.

The chief wants to know how the hell we know that Maiden Broom has been paroled.

I tell him we have our sources.

"You damn well better have 'em. You've just accused the parole board of violating their own rules. Heads are gonna roll, either yours or theirs."

In the story, we didn't mention what the guy at the board said about Maiden being only one of many felons who got paroled without the victims' families, or anyone else, being notified. I told Leighton we could save that one for the Monday paper, once she has a chance to confirm the names her source gave her.

When I impart this bit of information to the chief, he's quiet for a few seconds.

"Are you shitting me?" he asks at last. "Man, those people really fucked up."

I suggest that he might want to consider releasing Simms on bond as soon as possible, something that should have been done long before now.

"Yeah, I think that asshole in the mayor's office will sign off on that now," L.D. says.

I ask him how the manhunt, or now probably woman hunt, for the Dogtown Slasher is going.

"We're on it," he says. "Don't worry about that. We're gonna catch her. It's just a matter of time."

He remembers something else he wants to rag on me about.

"What about that thing at the joint on Main Street. Were you going to tell me about that?"

"Would you have given a shit if I had?"

"We're always interested in useful information from the public, even journalists," he says.

I let that slide and tell L.D. I'll get back with him in a couple of hours so we can tell our readers that Sly Simms is a free man, plus give him an update on the search for Maiden Broom.

"I might not be available," he says. "Thanks to you, it's going to be a busy day."

When the phone buzzed, I took it into the living room. When I come back to bed, Cindy's awake.

"If you worked a normal job," she says, "you might not get woken up before sunrise on a Sunday morning."

I tell her there might be an opening or two at the state parole board soon.

✦ ✦ ✦

ABE SPENT the night with Stella Stellar. The two of them meet us at Joe's. R.J. and Andy are already there when we arrive. We have to wait twenty minutes for a table, since the COVID rules say the place can only be about half full.

Andy thanks me for not mentioning his name in my retelling of his friend's encounter with the knife-wielding redhead.

"That was you?" Cindy says to her brother. "Dammit, Andy, when are you gonna stop fooling around? You're too old for that crap. Grace is going to cut your dick off while you're sleeping one of these days."

Andy protests that it wasn't him, it was his friend who was on the make.

"Oh, and you were just there to keep temptation from rearing its ugly head, I guess."

"Exactly."

"They ought to neuter all of you when you hit sixty," she mutters, looking at me.

I tell her that time will take care of that.

"Eventually," she says, stifling a smile.

It amazes me that Andy and Grace, who grew up with all of us on the Hill, are still married. They've separated at least three times, but it never lasts. My first, second, and third wives were more than willing to see our marriages sail off into the sunset.

"She says she's waiting for me to die so she can inherit the hardware store," he explains. Whatever it takes.

We're still on our second bloodies and thinking about taking the server's suggestion and ordering solid nourishment when my cell buzzes.

I recognize Marcus Green's number.

"Just wanted you to know," he says when I pick up, "that we won't have to worry about getting Sylvester Simms out of jail anymore."

"They turned him loose already?"

"Didn't have to. He set himself free."

"He escaped?"

"Yeah. He escaped all right. Escaped jail. Escaped the planet Earth. Escaped the goddamn need to keep breathing."

Sometime early this morning, after I'd posted the story I figured would finally convince the mayor, the chief, and everyone else that they had the wrong sap in jail, Sly Simms somehow got hold of a cord that was long enough to tie one end around his neck and the other to a light fixture.

The guards found him hanging there an hour later.

"Dammit, Willie. I told him to just be patient, that we'd get him out of there. He just couldn't wait, I guess."

No one has ever accused Marcus of being a sentimental slob, but this has cracked even his cast-iron veneer.

"Somebody's going to pay for this," he says. Neither of us knows who exactly that might be, since if Simms had any family at all, they sure as shit didn't show up when Marcus was trying to get him out of the slammer. The cynic in me says grieving half-brothers, desolate first cousins, and inconsolable aunts and uncles will come scurrying out of the woodwork once the scent of cash is in the air.

At any rate, Sylvester Simms is dead, probably a day before he would have walked out of jail on bond, facing nothing more serious than whatever they give you for picking a dead man's pockets.

I excuse myself, explaining the reason for my absence and imposing on Custalow to give Cindy a ride home. She offers to come with me, but I tell her I'm not even sure where exactly I'm going, just that there's a story out there.

I call Peachy, who confirms what Marcus Green just told me. She says she imagines the chief is in his office by now. Sunday's shot to hell, although not as much as it's ruined for the late Mr. Simms.

It's easy to get in to see L.D. today, since his pit-bull aide isn't guarding the door.

"Don't start," he says as I walk in. "Don't say a damn word. Jesus, what a fucking mess."

He's preparing a statement for the news media, which he intends to address at three o'clock.

"Will the mayor be there?"

He snorts.

"No. His Highness has decided that it'd be better if I address this one myself. He'll probably call his own press conference tomorrow. That's the one where he'll express shock and dismay over the way a man was held for more than a week when the evidence pointed to his obvious innocence."

"But you've got Stefanski to back you up," I say, referencing the mayor's insistence that Simms was the Slasher, case closed, in a conversation L.D. made sure his chief deputy overheard.

The chief looks up.

"Here's hoping," he says.

I ask him what he means.

"Fuckin' Stefanski would like to move his ass into my office," he says. "This would be a great opportunity for him to do just that. I hope he doesn't come down with a case of amnesia."

The chief and our mayor, with his eyes on the lieutenant governor's job, probably don't exchange Christmas cards. The latter wanted to pin the tail on L.D. for last year's shitstorm that led to most of our Confederate monuments disappearing. The chief saved his job with a nifty piece of blackmail, but Hizzoner hasn't forgotten.

It will not play well with the general public if it becomes known that our mayor stonewalled pursuing alternative theories as to who's been knocking off Richmonders this new year. But L.D.'s worried that his ear witness might sell him out.

"Stefanski doesn't seem like that much of a snake," I observe, trying to make the chief feel better.

"Oh, he's got some fangs," L.D. replies.

He says he won't lay the blame on the mayor for the time being.

"I just want to see which way he's goin' to spin it. If he wants to take his share of the shit sandwich, that'll be fine. Otherwise, well, we'll see how it plays out."

I remind the chief that he does have a document, signed by him and Stefanski, spelling out the mayor's intent, which seems to make him feel marginally better.

I take my leave, promising to be there at three.

"I can't wait," he says.

"You know Marcus Green will be there. I'm sure he's going to want some answers."

"What that son of a bitch wants is some money. Ah, hell. Somebody deserves some money for this screwup. If I had it to do over again, I'd tell the mayor to go fuck himself and push the commonwealth's attorney to let the guy post bond."

✦ ✦ ✦

I CALL Sarah, who thought she was going to spend a rare quiet Sunday at home with her new hubby.

"I'm on my way in," she says, despite my assurances that the story is going to write itself and probably won't need any lawyering.

Job One is to get something on the website about Sylvester Simms's suicide. That, of course, will all be updated after the chief meets the media at three.

That only leaves the story half-told though. We know who didn't kill four Richmonders. The cops should have a pretty damn good idea who to look for. However, until Maiden Broom is somehow unearthed, we have a stone-cold, apparently demented killer on the loose.

Plus I expect to hear very soon from someone in a position of power on the state parole board, no doubt denying everything and threatening major legal action. The Grimm Group's lawyer will not be amused.

We have a decent description of the woman from the Pratt girl and from Andy Peroni's tomcatting buddy, although the hair color was different. Anna Pratt said the woman who tried to hurt her was driving a white Honda or Toyota. I call Andy, who's on his way back from brunch, and ask him what I forgot to ask before: What kind of car?

As a matter of fact, I tell my old friend, I want to talk to this guy. Like today.

He says he'll ask his friend as soon as he can talk to him outside the guy's wife's earshot.

"Do it now," I tell Andy. "I don't give a damn how you do it, but I need to talk to him. Tell him if he doesn't talk to me, when I find out who he is, and I will, I'm going to use his name in the next story I write about this crap."

"You wouldn't."

"I might. At least, you'd better convince him I'm that kind of a son of a bitch."

"Man," Andy says, "see if I ever give you a hot tip again."

I apologize but explain that it's a wee bit important that we find this maniac as soon as possible.

Andy says he'll have the guy call me.

While I'm waiting for that, I get the call I'm expecting from the parole board.

The woman on the other end, who might not have a job much longer, says there is no truth in the "false allegations" in today's paper.

"So Maiden Broom is safely tucked away in her cell at the women's prison?"

"We cannot comment on that," the voice says. "We do not comment on a prisoner's status."

"Let me ask you this," I reply. "Can you verify the status of any of the following prisoners?" And I tick off the five names that Leighton wormed out of her enamored source yesterday.

A silence follows.

"Any of them?" I ask.

Crickets. Then, it sounds as if she is talking to someone else in the background.

"We will have to call you back on those names," she says, "but I can assure you that the parole board has followed the letter of the law in dealing with these individuals."

"Including notifying families of the victims when one of them is released?"

I advise her to answer that one carefully, since she might have to defend it later to somebody a lot more important than a tired-ass night cops reporter.

"You are going to be hearing from our lawyer," she says.

"So I'll take that as a 'no.'"

She hangs up.

Sarah has arrived.

I walk over and tell her that she can tell the Grimm Group's legal brain trust that we're not going to have a lot to worry about, suit-wise.

✦ ✦ ✦

THE PRESS conference is a shit show.

All the TV types, cranky already about having to rouse themselves on a Sunday afternoon, are asking L.D. all kinds of rude questions. The guy who covers the legislature for the *Washington Post* is there too. He asks the chief if he was under any orders from higher up to stick with the story that Sylvester Simms was the perpetrator of the first three murders.

L.D. swallows hard and walks a tightrope between dumping the whole hot mess in the mayor's lap and falling on the sword himself.

"Everyone was in agreement that the late Mr. Simms was the logical suspect in the killings of Harlan Bell and Jack and Sheila McCaskill," he says. "Obviously, in light of what we've since learned, Mr. Simms probably did nothing more criminal than steal from a dead man. If the newspaper had run this morning's story a day earlier, this tragedy could have been avoided."

Well played, L.D. Lay the blame on the lazy press. We're always the usual suspect when you need to deflect blame. Ignore the fact that I told you three days ago that Sly Simms had a believable alibi covering the time when the McCaskills were butchered, or the fact I've been telling you repeatedly how unlikely a murder suspect Simms was.

I bite my tongue. The chief's going to catch enough hell without me piling on.

I hear a familiar voice.

"Chief Jones," the reporter from the alternative weekly booms out, "do you think race played any part in this whole sorry mess?"

L.D. is stumped, as are we all.

"I mean," the guy continues, "would Sylvester Simms have been held in jail so long in the face of compelling evidence as to his innocence if he had been white."

Jesus Christ. The penny drops. Sylvester Simms, in the only photo we were able to get before they put him in jail, might have looked African American. I mean, he's darker complected than yours truly, but that's probably because his face had been so weather-blasted after decades left out in the heat and cold.

Having actually talked with the man, I believe I am on safe ground when I say that Sly Simms was of European descent.

The chief explains this to the reporter, who tries to brazen it out by asking, "Are you sure?"

"What a dumbass," I hear one of the good-hair TV folks mutter. This is the definition of being called ugly by a frog.

L.D. just stares at the confused reporter, who doesn't say anything else, and the press conference soon, and mercifully for the chief, concludes.

Back at the office, I plug a few quotes from L.D. into the story and pass the bullshit denial from the parole board to Leighton, who is in the office on a Sunday plugging away at the mystery parolees story like she can smell Pulitzer. By the time I'm done, I get a call from a number I don't recognize.

"Yeah," the voice says, "um, Andy Peroni said I had to call you. Look, you got to keep me out of this."

I assure Andy's friend that I won't use his name, that I don't even officially know his name, although I've pretty much figured it out by now, being familiar with most of Andy's running mates.

All I want to know, I tell him, is as much as he can tell me about the woman he tried to pick up.

"What kind of car?"

"I'm pretty sure it was a Toyota Corolla. White."

"And you told Andy that she had red hair, but you thought it was a wig."

"Yeah. It was pretty good, but I'm sure it was a wig. Maybe to make her look younger."

He says he figures she was about fifty, "but real fit, pretty hot, really."

He's already been apprised by Andy that the woman who waved a big-ass knife in his face might be the Dogtown Slasher.

"Scared the shit out of me," he says. "I might have been killed."

Might yet, I think, if your wife finds out you're chasing pussy on boys' night out.

"Is there anything else you remember about her? Anything she said or did that might be helpful?"

He says he can't remember anything, but then he does.

"I asked her where she lived, and she just kind of winked and said 'all over.' Then I started talking about restaurants, just to keep the conversation going, and she said she didn't get out much, but that she gets takeout sometimes."

"Did she say where?"

"Damn, I wish I could remember. Let me think. Can I email it to you? It'd be more, you know, private."

I tell him that'd be fine, but I expect his memory to come back to him sometime soon.

"You're not gonna give me up to the cops, are you?"

"Not if I don't have to."

I hear him groan, and he says he'll rack his brain. I tell him to rack away.

While waiting for the genius's brainstorm, I make a call to the Pratt residence.

Chip Pratt answers. He, like most of Richmond, has gotten the news now that the police have been holding the wrong psychopath. Most of them probably got it from TV or the Internet, rather than the source, aka me.

He says it's scared him more than his daughter, who, he says, thinks that it's "kind of cool" that a serial killer targeted her.

"We're keeping her pretty close to home," he says.

I ask him if it would be OK if I came by and talked with Anna and also with Wilson Pratt Senior.

"Because of that thing in Staunton way back when?"

"I just want to find out if there's anything he can tell me."

"Damn," he says. "Talk about holding a grudge."

He does accommodate me and tells me I can come out to his house. His father's there "but I don't know if we want Anna talking to you. I'd kind of like to keep her out of the spotlight until they catch the bitch."

✦ ✦ ✦

LEIGHTON SAYS the parole board flack has given her the same line she gave me.

"I think she figured my chain was more jerkable than yours, me being a poor little girl and all," Leighton says, grinning like a wolf surveying a lamb chop.

I'm sure the parole board lady will be disabused of that fantasy.

When I get to the Pratts, Wilson Sr. is sitting in the den, waiting for me. Anna, no doubt at her parents' insistence, is a no-show.

The elder Pratt seems as mystified as anyone over the fact that he and his family seem to have become targets of a woman he helped put away more than three decades ago.

"I remember the case very well," he says. "The whole community was in an uproar. The Brooms were well-liked.

The jury didn't stay out that long, maybe overnight. I do remember the girl was somewhat distraught, but there wasn't much doubt she was guilty. It was a slam dunk."

He says he isn't leaving the house much these days, and when he does, he's packing, like just about everyone else in town but with more reason than most.

"And to try to take it out on my granddaughter," he says, shaking his head. "I guess she figured that would be worse than killing me. To me it would have been. Hell, when you're dead, you're dead."

I ask him about the brother, Beverley Junior, about whom I know little.

"Never a trace of him, far as I know," he says. "People figured she probably killed him, too, but nobody ever found a body."

As I'm leaving, he says the reappearance of Maiden Broom caught him flat-footed.

I tell him I'm sure he oversaw the imprisonment and even eventual execution of more than a few miscreants over the decades.

"Oh, yes," he says. "Three of them were executed, one by the electric chair and two by lethal injection. But I don't think any of them ever sent me a letter, like Maiden Broom did."

I stop walking.

He says he only remembered it today, when it became clear that the woman he prosecuted more than thirty-two years ago might be the same one who tried to hurt his granddaughter.

"It must have been twenty years ago," he says. "It was a postcard, from the women's prison. All it said was, 'Thinking of you,' with her name signed at the bottom. I thought about turning it over to the folks at the prison, but then I just let it pass."

When I get back to the Prestwould, I check my email. There's a message from Andy Peroni's computer. In it, Andy says he's acting as proxy for his friend, who did remember something. The woman with the knife, he recalled, said she got takeout sometimes from O'Toole's, a joint on Forest Hill Avenue with which I have had a passing acquaintance over the years.

OK. That's something. Not something I can write about, but it might be worth giving L.D. Jones a heads-up. O'Toole's, the place Andy's friend remembered, is a Richmond institution that's been around almost as long as I have. It's in a part of Dogtown that is home to middle-class folks; even a few journalists can afford to live there. The area is full of leafy streets, spacious parks, and brick and wood-frame homes aging gracefully. Not far from there, though, is a part of Richmond that mostly is mentioned in the Police and Crime News section. I remember one day last fall, three separate bodies were discovered in the area south of the Midlothian Turnpike and west of US 1, maybe a mile as the crow flies from O'Toole's.

So, if Maiden Broom, a relative newcomer to our fair city, has been getting takeout from O'Toole's, chances are she's holed up somewhere in the vicinity.

I call L.D., who's getting used to me disturbing his peace.

"That might not mean anything," he says. "I mean, she has a damn car. She could just like the food there."

Still he concedes that it's something to think about.

He says the mayor has not communicated with him yet about the Sylvester Simms mess.

"He's happy to let me stew in that juice all by myself," he says. "Long as he doesn't try to pile on, he'll be OK. Hell, I hope he does get his ass elected lieutenant governor. Then he won't be mayor anymore. Somebody else's problem."

I point out that, if he's elected lieutenant governor, he'd be a heartbeat away from the governor's mansion.

"Yeah," the chief says, "but he won't get to spend all his time up my ass."

CHAPTER THIRTEEN

Monday, January 18

THE CHIEF'S concerns about Hizzoner are justified.

The mayor releases a statement decrying the failure of Richmond's police department to realize that evidence pointed away from the now-deceased Sylvester Simms as the Dogtown Slasher and toward somebody who's still out there wielding a big-ass knife.

By the time Sarah calls and tells me about it, it's after nine, so I figure L.D.'s already at work.

Across the room, Cindy's working the phone like a rented mule. With the possibility of a vaccine against Mr. COVID hanging in the air like a mirage in the desert, everybody's trying to find a way to get stuck. The first ones to be vaccinated are supposed to be those over seventy-five, health-care workers, or people in much worse shape than either Cindy or me.

"Does smoking Camels put me at the front of the line?" I ask.

She doesn't bother to answer.

The rush is on though. Nothing makes people crazier, Cindy included, than thinking they're going to be left out, that everybody but them is on the road to a safe, no-mask future.

Cindy got an email from a friend who said "they" were taking reservations for vaccinations, but every time she calls the number the city provided, she either is cut off or gets a message saying call back later.

"We'll get it when we get it," I advise her. Normally I am not the voice of reason in our household, but my beloved has, I think, been driven around the bend by a year of lockdown. My only concern is getting Peggy on the list. Nobody knows whether the stuff can bite you a second time.

I tell her that I have to leave, that I need to have a meeting with the chief. Usually this would be met with some resistance, Monday being one of my two alleged days off. She just waves me away and continues cursing her phone.

✦ ✦ ✦

L.D. AGREES to meet me at Perly's for coffee.

"I knew he'd screw me," the chief says when he joins me at a back booth.

"So is your backup plan going to work?"

He nods.

"Yeah, it'll work. I had a long talk with Stefanski. I convinced him that it'd be in his best interests to not develop a case of amnesia. I also reminded him that he signed a statement verifying what we both heard.

"Stefanski's twenty years younger than me," L.D. adds. "I intimated to him that I was considering retirement in the near future, and that his support on this delicate issue would more or less ensure that he followed in my footsteps."

"So he went for that?"

L.D. frowns.

"What do you mean, 'went for'? You think I'm conning Stefanski?"

I explain that I've always thought L.D., despite his grumbling and threats to quit, would be carried out of his job feet-first.

"Nah, it ain't like that," he says.

He takes a sip of coffee and adds, "But I didn't say exactly when I was going to retire."

I ask the chief what his next move is.

"Well, I could go to Hizzoner and point out the fact that not only is he a lying bastard, but that I have a witness to that fact. But why do that when I can fuck him publicly, and maybe save the state from being stuck with him as lieutenant governor, and maybe governor someday?"

I tell him that I thought he'd said he would be glad to have the mayor off his ass rather than serving three more years as the city's top executive.

"Yeah, I thought about that, but I figure he's going to spend a lot of his energy the next three years just trying to cover his ass after you write the true story about what happened with Sylvester Simms."

Talk about a win-win. L.D. saves his job, I get a hell of a story, and Jimbo Stefanski maybe gets to be chief some-day soon. Maybe.

The chief reaches in his shirt pocket and produces the signed document detailing what he and his deputy chief heard.

It's about as easy a story as I've ever had dumped in my lap.

✦ ✦ ✦

BACK AT the work factory, I tell Wheelie and Sarah about the story I'm about to lay on our readers.

The mayor's flack, when I call, says the man has no comment.

Wheelie says we need to get it on the website as soon as possible. I tell him there's no hurry, that no one but us has a shot at this one.

Of course, I'm wrong. I do file the story placing much of the blame for the Sylvester Simms fuckup on the well-dressed shoulders of the man who would be lieutenant governor. And then Sarah calls me to her office.

"Looks like the mayor's not the only one the chief screwed," she says. She points to the TV screen, where L.D. and Jimbo Stefanski are telling the viewers about Hizzoner's role in that disaster.

"Good thing you filed it in a hurry," Wheelie says. "I think we scooped TV by about five minutes."

I say a few bad words and call the chief's number. No surprise, he's not available at present.

It doesn't take a genius to figure out that the chief wanted as much exposure as he could get, although a less duplicitous man might have at least given his favorite print reporter an exclusive. If I could tell Jimbo something right now, it would be to not be making plans to move into the big chair anytime soon, and to watch his back.

After I've taken a smoke break to calm down, it's time to start trying to dig a little deeper into the enigma that is Maiden Broom.

Leighton has been going after anyone she can find at the state parole board, whose officials are keeping a very low profile this morning.

She manages to contact two other victims' families who, like Carson Broom, were never informed that their beloveds' killers had been paroled.

"They didn't have a clue until the story ran in the paper about Maiden Broom. They were pretty pissed."

She finally gets a high-ranking official at the parole board to pick up her phone. The official vows that the board has done nothing wrong but does a little fancy dancing when asked about the victims' families. One of the newly freed, it turns out, was denied parole three months ago but then, upon further review, was granted it a month later. The family had a representative at the first meeting but didn't know about the second one.

Leighton finally gets her reluctant source to reveal that Maiden Broom was released from the state women's prison in Goochland on Dec. 30, almost three weeks ago. In the process, she discovered one of those quirks that get slipped into state law while nobody's looking: The parole board's records are not subject to Freedom of Information rules, which are meant to keep public officials from doing crazy shit under the cover of darkness.

"Still there's got to be some kind of record of who she would be staying with," I observe. "She couldn't have just been allowed to disappear into the woodwork."

"I'm aware of that," Leighton says. "Do you think I'm an idiot? I've got it. According to the parole board, she was given over to the custody of her first cousin."

"What's his name."

"James Caldwell."

"Where does this James Caldwell live?"

She reads it to me.

"Are you sure?"

She repeats it. I tell her it's exactly one digit removed from her uncle Carson Broom's address.

"Jesus H. Christ. The place where she killed her parents? Damn. Nobody checked the address to see if it was real?"

That seems to be the case. I tell Leighton how unlikely it is that Maiden's uncle would have had anything to do with providing safe shelter for the niece he heartily wanted to see imprisoned for the rest of her natural life and then burn in hell.

"Well, call him and find out for sure."

I congratulate my young peer for managing to shed a little light on something that someone wanted kept dark as a coal mine at midnight and assure her that I'm going to be giving Carson Broom a call as soon as our conversation is over.

"Anything else about this guy, Caldwell?" I ask.

"Not that I'm aware of, just an address. He had to show some kind of identification though."

Maiden is due for a meeting with her parole officer a month after her release, which would be sometime next week.

Smart money says she'll be a no-show.

I call the chief to tell him what a no-account backstabbing SOB he is for giving my story to every TV station in town.

"Where the fuck does it say this is your story?" he asks in a tone not the least bit apologetic. "It's my story, and I can share it with anybody I damn well please. I'm a lot more interested in getting it out everywhere I can than in hurting your little snowflake feelings."

I tell him that I hope he doesn't expect any favors from me in the near or distant future.

"Favors?" he says when he stops laughing. "The next favor I get from you will be the first one. You're lucky I didn't just take it to the TV folks and let you get it from them."

We part without wishing each other a nice day.

Next up: Carson Broom.

He actually answers his phone when I call. He is somewhat apoplectic when I tell him the address that is allegedly now home to his recently sprung relative.

"That's ridiculous," he sputters. "That address doesn't exist."

Then he has another thought.

"You don't think she'll be coming back here, do you?"

I can't in all honesty tell the man to relax. He would seem to be a prime target for his niece. I do mention that most of the mayhem Maiden has apparently been inflicting has been on the good folks of Richmond.

He mumbles something about maybe going over to his sister's house for a few days. I voice my approval for that idea.

"Do you know anybody named James Caldwell?" I ask. He doesn't.

I tell him to stay safe.

"Just catch the bitch," he replies.

✦ ✦ ✦

NONE OF the good people at the parole board want to comment on the record, and damn few are willing to talk off the record, although it is becoming clear that some of the people involved with what passes for justice are not exactly thrilled with the board's recent penal largesse. Leighton has been able to contact another couple of victims' families, also, and they're not even a little bit happy.

The governor's office hasn't weighed in yet, not surprising since most of the parole board came on during his watch. It's butt-covering time.

The mayor doesn't take long to respond to the chief's revelation that Hizzoner was the driving force behind keeping Sylvester Simms locked up.

He doesn't recall having any conversation with L.D. about Simms. As a matter of fact, he doesn't remember even talking with his chief of police in the last month or so. So it'll be his word against L.D.'s and Stefanski's. A smarter mayor might have pussy-footed around and said that he did recall some kind of conversation with his chief, but that he certainly didn't in any way condone keeping an innocent man behind bars.

Maybe, when he has a chance to confer with his brain trust, if he has one, they'll come up with something that's a little more believable. Maybe tomorrow he'll remember. Maybe he'll just say that L.D. and Stefanski must have misunderstood his intent, or some such shit.

"He's only been running for lieutenant governor for, what, less than a week," Sally Velez says, "and he's already stepped on his dick."

There's plenty to write about, even if the chief has given the good-hair folks the same "exclusive" he gave me. I update my later post with the mayor's lame-ass denial. Leighton asks me to take a look at what she's written about the parole board, and then it's time to hit the bricks. Sally wants to know when I'm coming back, and I remind her that this is Monday, a day for which I am not being paid.

"Oh," she says, "I thought you were on the seven-day plan."

Before I leave, I see that Sarah and Wheelie are in his office with the door closed. Closed doors are not usually good news these days.

"Did you hear about the layoffs in Roanoke?" Callie Ann Boatwright asks as I'm pondering whether to knock on my ultimate editor's door.

I decide it's probably not a good time to check in with my bosses. Maybe they can't fire me if they can't find me.

✦ ✦ ✦

I CHECK in with Cindy.

"Want to go for a drive?" I ask.

"Sure," she says. "Anything to get my mind off goddamn COVID hell."

She's had a busy but nonproductive day. Four times she was allowed to register for vaccination appointments for us, only to have the website then tell her the time for which she was approved was not available. And then the website crashed.

She stops bitching long enough to ask me where we're going.

O'Toole's, I reply.

When I pick her up outside the Prestwould, she looks a little irritated.

"I spent the whole damn day on this crap," she says as we're headed toward Dogtown. "I have yet to speak to one live human being."

I'm thinking live human beings would be wise to steer clear of Lucinda Peroni Black at the moment. I remind her that neither of us is old enough to qualify for the vaccine yet, but she keeps getting emails from know-it-alls who tell her they're taking appointments at the Diamond, or the racetrack or, for all I know, some damn alley in the projects.

"I just don't want to get left out," she says.

Then she thinks to ask: "Why O'Toole's?"

I tell her what her brother's tomcatting friend said.

"He said she got takeout from there?"

"Yeah. So I thought they might remember her, that maybe she's staying somewhere in the neighborhood."

She turns to me.

"Don't we have a police force to check this crap out? Somewhere there's a cop eating a donut while you play Dick Tracy on your day off."

I concede that we do, indeed, have a police force. I add that I've already made L.D. aware of this possible connection.

"And?"

"He said they'd look into it, but L.D. isn't much for following up on the leads I pass his way. Plus he's spending half his time trying to keep the mayor from pinning the donkey tail on him."

I tell her about the chief's little revelation that probably has put the man who would be lieutenant governor's ass in a sling.

"Well," Cindy says, "I think it'd be a pleasant change once in a while if you were able to write a nice, safe story about the police arresting a suspect instead of putting your own neck on the line."

Where, I ask her, is the fun in that?

As I've been abducted more than once over the years and have suffered the indignity, at one point, of having half my ear shot off in pursuit of the truth, I see her point though.

O'Toole's has been there since the 1960s. It is an old favorite of mine that might never be the kind of joint that's written up in foodie magazines. Me, I'll take Spaghetti O'Toole over lamb belly with enoki mushrooms.

Back in the day, happy hour at O'Toole's often became happy night. Every time I go there, I wonder why I don't go more often, but then laziness sets in and I wind up dining at the usual suspects, where the waitress asks only one question: "The usual?"

The place hasn't changed much. Various family crests, although none for the Blacks, adorn the wall. The gang at the U-shaped bar looks about the same as it did last time I was in here.

We take one of the booths next to the side street. We're here in time for either a very early supper or a very late lunch, so seating's no problem. Cindy orders a grilled tuna sandwich while I decide to go the healthy route.

"A Philly steak sub with onion rings?" Cindy asks as the waitress departs. "Sure you don't want some gravy with that?"

We're into our entrees, with Cindy stealing some of my onion rings, when I ask our server, a young woman dressed in a black uniform, if I can speak with the manager.

I see frown wrinkles above her mask.

"Is anything wrong?"

Not in the least, I assure her. I just have a question.

A couple of minutes later, the guy running the show comes over to our table. He nods like he remembers me from times past.

"What's the problem?"

I tell him there isn't one, and then I tell him why I'm here, other than the delicious steak sub and superb onion rings.

"She said she got takeout from here?" he asks.

I describe her to the guy, noting that her red hair might or might not have been a wig. I show him the very sketchy sketch that Handley Pace, our artist, did for the paper, based on a high-school yearbook photo and the descriptions from Anna Pratt and Andy Peroni's friend.

"She'd be about fifty years old. I'm told she is kind of intense."

"Yeah, I'd have guessed that," the manager says, looking at the drawing. Like most of Richmond, he's been following the Dogtown Slasher saga.

"So you work for the newspaper?" he says. "I get most of my news on TV or the Internet. No offense."

None taken, I assure him. I can tell that Cindy wants to take him to task for his lack of support for his hometown rag, but I squeeze her knee and she stifles the urge.

He says he thinks the woman in the sketch looks familiar.

"Let me check with Richard."

Richard is a kid who doesn't look old enough to be employed at a restaurant. He is responsible for, among other things, hustling food to people who come in for takeout.

The kid looks at the sketch and says he might remember seeing her.

"I think she was with some dude," he says. "They ordered burgers, I think."

I ask him if he saw what kind of car they were driving. He's not sure. When I ask him if it might have been a white Toyota, he shrugs and says it could have been.

He says he thinks the woman has picked up a couple of times "both in the last two weeks, I think." He doesn't remember her saying anything beyond "keep the change."

We finish our dinner. I try to call L.D., but he's not answering, so I leave a text message, emphasizing the wisdom in making Dogtown Ground Zero in the department's search for Maiden Broom.

As we're leaving, the manager comes over.

"Hey," he says. "Do you think you all could stop calling her the Dogtown Slasher? Not too good for business."

I remind him that all publicity is good.

He doesn't agree.

I tell him I'll talk to my editors about it.

✦ ✦ ✦

CINDY IS driving us back toward the Prestwould when I get a text message.

It's from Sarah, and there's an attachment.

"Check this out," reads the text.

The photo is of a woman's neck and upper chest. She's wearing a necklace. I look more closely, not quite believing what I'm seeing.

"What?" Cindy asks.

She pulls over into a no-parking space on Broad Street.

"Holy shit," she says when she's stopped and I show her the attachment. "Is that what I think it is?"

I tell her I'm pretty sure it is.

Someone has made some kind of demented jewelry out of what appear to be human fingers. They are of various sizes and colors and look a bit worse for the wear from having been unattached from the rest of their human bodies for a while.

"Ewww," responds my beloved. "That is beyond sick."

That's not the worst part of it, I tell her.

She asks me what I mean.

"Count the fingers," I reply.

She does.

"Ten. So what?"

I count them off. One from Harlan Bell. Two from Jack McCaskill. Three from Dr. Cartwright.

And four more.

What's left of my "off" day just got shot to hell.

CHAPTER FOURTEEN

Tuesday, January 19

AFTER SOME waffling yesterday on the part of Benson Stine, our spineless publisher, we were allowed to run the picture of the finger necklace. Its provenance is uncertain, although there's little doubt about whose neck that is. L.D.'s crack crew later determined that it was sent from a burner phone. It appears to be nonresponsive now and probably sleeps with the James River fishes.

By the time the chief responded to my text, I was two-thirds of the way through a first draft of a story that told last night's online freeloaders and this morning's print readers that a woman resembling Maiden Broom had been seen around O'Toole's, and that somebody had sent a photo to the newspaper that was best not viewed over breakfast. The story noted that three of the Slasher's victims had a total of six of their fingers lopped off, and that the picture shows a necklace holding four more.

L.D. must have known it was a fool's errand to ask me to hold this one until the cops could investigate, especially after he burned me on the scoop that has revealed our mayor to be less than an honest man. Still I guess he had to try.

I suggested again to the chief that it might be a good idea to put some more shoe leather in the general vicinity of O'Toole's.

"What the fuck for?" he said. "You've already told her we know where she is. If she's got a brain and any access to the news, she knows we're going to be all over that neighborhood. She's probably on the run now, anywhere but Dogtown."

Nevertheless I'm sure the constabulary will be dogging Dogtown for the time being. Better late than never.

I got home after ten and gave Cindy the short version of how I wasted the rest of my "off" day.

"But there haven't been any more bodies around here that aren't accounted for, are there?" she asked.

Actually there was one poor sap whose remains were found yesterday snagged on the rocks in the James down below the pedestrian bridge at Browns Island, but since his kayak was found not far away, the assumption is that our watery playground has claimed another overenthusiastic, underprepared soul. Kayaking in January sounds like a death wish to me.

And, when I asked Peachy to check, she got back to me and said the corpse was in possession of all its fingers, frozen though they were.

So the mayor's trying to save his political ass, the parole board is in deep shit, and there's probably a corpse out there somewhere missing four fingers. And a woman with what seems to be the world's largest and longest-lasting grudge is, as they say, at large.

"Sounds like you'd better get some sleep," Cindy said. "Tomorrow's going to be a busy day."

"At least I won't be working for free."

"Poor baby," she said as she wandered into the kitchen to feed the cats. She didn't sound sincere.

✦ ✦ ✦

THIS MORNING, I drop by to see how Andi's doing. I've only talked with her once since I was given the good news that William is going to have a little sibling.

My daughter is still working from home most days. She says she's glad she's not in the food and beverage business. A couple of waitress friends tested positive.

"I do kind of miss the excitement though," she says.

I suggest that perhaps spending twenty-four hours of most days with her son might be a bit much.

"Are you kidding?" she says. "He's the best thing that's ever happened to me."

Sure, I reply. But even Christmas would get old if it came every day.

She's quiet for a minute.

Then she nods her head.

"Well, yeah. It will be nice to get a little normal back in our lives, I guess."

She says she's planning on getting the COVID vaccine, despite her delicate condition.

"I'm no math major," she says, "but I see all the shit that's happening to people who get infected, and it's kind of a no-brainer."

Not exactly, I correct her. Lots of people with no brains insist they won't take the shot.

She and Walter don't know the new baby's sex yet. She says it'll be spring sometime before they do.

"Do you care which it is?" I ask.

"Healthy," she replies.

She's a little on edge about the fact that we seem to have a crazed killer running loose out there.

"That picture in the paper," she says. "I mean, we don't get the paper edition of course, but I saw it online. Yecch!"

I tell Andi not to worry too much, that as far as I know, she has not managed to get on the shit list of a woman most of us outside the prison system have never even seen for the last thirty-some years.

✦ ✦ ✦

IT OCCURRED to me that I didn't have much information about the teenage Maiden Broom, so I have managed to get the names of a couple of her classmates at the last private school she was kicked out of before giving her parents forty whacks.

One of them has agreed to talk to me this morning, maybe because she lives in Illinois, outside the present range of Maiden's rampage.

The woman, who's fifty like the suspect herself, is a lawyer living in the Chicago suburbs. She insists that we not use her name or any other information about her "just in case."

"She was kind of scary," the old classmate says. "We were pretty close, I guess, but you knew not to cross her."

The day she got booted from the private school, over in West Virginia, for "borrowing" a classmate's car, my source says that she went to Maiden's room "to wish her well, I suppose."

"She had this kind of glazed look, like she was drunk, but I knew she hadn't been drinking. She said she was, and I'm paraphrasing here, but I think this is the gist of it, 'going to skin that bitch alive,' meaning the girl whose car she stole.

"I tried to talk to her, to tell her that the other girl, whom I knew really well, was just freaked because her car was stolen.

"And Maiden pointed her finger at me and accused me of taking the other girl's side. Said everybody was against her, just like her parents."

I asked the woman if Maiden talked much about her mother and father.

"Oh, all the time. She said they were evil. You've got to remember that you couldn't always take what Maiden said to the bank, but she intimated that they did things to her. Like, sexual things. She said that if it wasn't for her brother, she wouldn't have had a friend in the world.

"I told her that I thought that we were friends, and she just looked at me and said, 'For now.'"

I ask if she knew much about Maiden's brother.

"Just mostly what she told me, although he did come up one time to see her. They went off somewhere for the weekend. I don't think her folks ever came up except to drop her off and then pick her up when she got kicked out."

She said Beverley Junior, who went by Buddy, seemed "a little off. Like he never looked at you when he talked to you. He looked a lot like Maiden. You could tell they were brother and sister."

The woman says Maiden was a good student "when she put her mind to it" and was popular with the students from the local boys' school with whom she and her classmates had some social intercourse.

"She wasn't even sixteen yet then, I guess it was six months or so before she was supposed to have done what she did, but she'd, you know, been around the block once or twice."

She says Maiden's former classmates were shocked when they heard she was accused of hacking her parents to death "but when we talked about it, I think we all agreed that if there had been a category in the yearbook for 'Most Likely to Murder Your Parents,' Maiden would have been everybody's choice."

We talk awhile longer, but the woman doesn't seem to have any further light to shed on her old classmate.

Then, as I'm about to end our chat, she remembers something.

"That girl, Susan, the one whose car Maiden borrowed, stole, whatever, we used to exchange Christmas cards every year. One year, it was I think 2005 or 2006, because we'd just moved, she sent me a card, and in it she mentioned that she'd gotten a postcard a few days before. From Maiden Broom. All the card said was, 'Thinking of you. Maiden.' And the return address was that prison where she was being held."

My source says she's lost touch with the woman whose car Maiden took all those years ago.

"I think it kind of freaked her out, that Maiden knew where she lived. I mean, this was almost twenty years since that incident with the car. We've fallen out of touch, and I think Susan's moved a time or two since then, got divorced."

The woman is silent for a few seconds, then says she thinks she'll try to find Susan. I don't discourage the idea, but I tell the woman that Maiden was paroled less than three weeks ago and apparently has spent most of that time settling scores in the Richmond area.

"Still," she says, "I think I'll try to find her."

After a light lunch with Cindy, Butterball, and Rags, I give a call to the Pratt residence. Wilson Pratt Senior is home, and he's willing to talk to me, as long as it's not for attribution.

I tell him about the conversation I've just had with one of Maiden Broom's private-school acquaintances, and I ask him if at any time Maiden's lawyers brought up possible sexual abuse by her parents. I figure they must have been throwing out anything they could, hoping something would stick with the jury.

He's quiet for a long time. I let the silence work.

Then I hear him clear his throat.

"She said a lot of things. When she was interviewed by the police, she said some terrible things about Beverley and Connie."

"Did any of that come out in court?"

Pratt Senior says that it did not. The defense attorney chose not to have Maiden testify.

"The way I remember it, he felt like it would hurt her case if she got up there and started ranting about things that nobody on the jury, hell, nobody in the community, would believe. Plus she had a hair-trigger temper. I guess that goes without saying. A good prosecutor probably could have gotten her to say she was glad her parents were dead if he'd pushed her very hard."

The defense attorney was no prize, Pratt says, "So, in all honesty, she might not have gotten the very best counsel she could have gotten."

I can't argue with that. Seems like a person on trial for murdering her parents might want to use every excuse in the book, whether there was any truth in them or not.

I thank Mr. Pratt and ask him if he's been keeping a low profile.

"Oh, hell yeah," he says. "My son and daughter-in-law won't let me outside the house. And Anna hasn't been back to school since all this started."

✦ ✦ ✦

I HAVE time before the night cops beat starts to take a leisurely drive through the part of Dogtown where Maiden Broom has reportedly been seen.

It's kind of a fool's errand, but I turn down one of the side streets next to O'Toole's and start circling around, never going more than four blocks from the eatery itself. There are plenty of nice old houses with big shade trees now bare in the January cold, although the farther away I get, the less charming they seem to be. The place looks very peaceful, and I don't see any signs of a crazed killer or even a white Corolla.

I turn onto a street that borders a part of Reedy Creek that's been converted into a big concrete draining ditch. That's when I find out that my search has not gone unnoticed. As I'm turning back toward Forest Hill, a cop car comes wheeling up behind me, right on my bumper, with the blue light on. I run through possible offenses. I haven't had a drink today, I wasn't talking on my cell phone, I'm pretty sure I was doing twenty-two in a twenty-five.

And out pops Gillespie. Chauncey Gillespie, donut eater par excellence, exits his squad car and waddles up to my window. I sit with both hands on the steering wheel, being at least partially African American. Call me overly cautious.

"Oh, fuck. It's just goddamn Willie Black," I hear him say to his partner after he leans in the window.

Apparently the chief has finally seen the wisdom in concentrating the cops' search for Maiden Broom in Dogtown.

Since I've been cruising the streets for the last fifteen minutes, Gillespie and his partner thought I looked suspicious, although I hardly fit the profile.

He asks me what I'm doing here. I tell him I'm looking for a lost cat. He advises me not to be a smart-ass, so I tell him that, since the police didn't seem interested in following up on the lead I gave L.D., I thought I'd do a little checking myself.

"Does it look like we're not working hard enough?" Gillespie asks. "And, oh yeah, your inspection sticker is out of date."

He doesn't write me a ticket, but he does give me a stern warning about not interfering with police business before he lets me go. I ask him if he's lost weight, and he calls me a smart-ass again.

✦ ✦ ✦

WHEN I get to the office, I call Marcus Green to find out what his legal strategy is for getting posthumous justice for Sylvester Simms.

Sure enough, the poor sap had a brother, and the brother came out of the woodwork as soon as it became known that Sly had offed himself while in police custody for a crime he obviously did not commit.

"Somebody's got some 'splainin' to do," says my favorite ambulance chaser. "Granted the late Mr. Simms is not going to be able to benefit from the city's fuckup, and it galls me to see money go to the same relative who probably wouldn't have pissed on him if he was on fire when he was alive, but justice must be served."

I observe that perhaps Marcus could put his cut of the settlement into some kind of fund in Mr. Simms's name, maybe to help one of the local homeless shelters. Marcus says he'll have to get back to me on that one.

"It's going to be fun to put the chief on the stand, if it comes to that," he adds, "so he can repeat what he said about the mayor putting the kibosh on releasing my late client."

We both agree that this isn't going to help Hizzoner's chances in the upcoming primary.

"Or his chances of getting reelected mayor," Marcus adds.

I reply that the bar for mayoral competency is pretty low in these parts. We've had some mayors who had worse problems than our present one. We're not Baltimore, but sometimes we get pretty close. It takes a lot to get unelected mayor of our fair city.

✦ ✦ ✦

BY THE time I get off the phone, there's excitement in the newsroom. As is usually the case these days, it's not good excitement.

A crowd has gathered around the desk of one of our most senior political reporters. Hayes has been here longer than me, which is saying something. He and I used to roam the legislative halls and close down the bars together before I got demoted to night cops.

As he dodged layoff after layoff, we all figured the brain trust around here decided he was just too damn essential to our institutional memory to be let go.

We were, of course, wrong. Bottom line—one, institutional memory—zero.

The kids like Leighton and Callie Ann Boatwright do a pretty good job wherever we put them, but it's all new to them. They don't know where the bodies are buried. They don't know the old stories. They haven't played enough poker with the pols and their flacks and the other political reporters. You mention a guy like Linwood Holton, who as a Republican in the early '70s was our most liberal governor since Reconstruction, and they say, in unison, "Who?" Then somebody has to explain how Democrats used to be Republicans in Virginia, and vice versa.

So we all drop by to say the meaningless crap you say when somebody gets the ax and it isn't you. I tell him nobody will ever again cover our feckless, conniving pols as well as he did, then see Leighton frowning as she stands off to one side.

"What the fuck was I supposed to say?" I ask her after my old drinking buddy has packed up his box and left the premises. "Besides, it's true. You'll never have the time to do what he did, since you'll be covering six other things at the same time. And you won't be staying up until three A.M. drinking and hearing all the stories."

"You mean the stories you can't write, or else they won't let you play with them anymore?"

Well, there was that. Some of Hayes's best stories were the ones he told me, the ones that never appeared in the paper.

"He said he might write a book," I offer.

"That'd be nice," Leighton says. "Maybe he could entitle it, 'All the shit I couldn't tell you when I was a reporter.'"

Cold. Maybe right, but cold nonetheless.

I do stop by Wheelie's office and ask him how he could let the Grimm Group take away his most senior reporter.

"Senior reporters make a pretty good salary," Wheelie says, not looking up. "You know that, right, Willie?"

It seems like a good time to leave Wheelie to his thoughts.

✦ ✦ ✦

Tomorrow's story says the police are conducting an extensive search for the Dogtown Slasher.

There's some background on the young Maiden Broom, compliments of her anonymous old classmate. And there's speculation on those four unidentified fingers in that image somebody sent us.

"Maybe she'll go into hiding, leave town, be somebody else's problem, now that the cops have a good idea where she is," Sarah Goodnight says.

"You really think so?"

She shakes her head.

The publisher drops by my desk to ask me how the "Slasher thing" is going. I tell Stine that it's going well, and then can't help adding that we are going to miss Hayes on the statehouse beat.

He doesn't say anything, just walks off.

"Brave man," Sally Velez says. "Keep it up and we'll be having a wake for you too."

We do have a wake for Hayes's career. We can't pack into Penny Lane like we'd do in normal times, but we all go over to Bootie Carmichael's condo to listen again to all those stories Hayes could never put into print.

Hayes says that, yeah, he might write a book.

That possibility must make a state senator or two a tad nervous.

CHAPTER FIFTEEN

Wednesday, January 20

WE GAVE Hayes a sendoff worthy of the man's contributions to print journalism. Well, we all got shitfaced on Bootie Carmichael's bourbon anyhow.

Sometime after two thirty, I drove Hayes home. This was not an extremely intelligent move, since I already have one fairly recent DWI on my record, but Hayes was a lot drunker than I was. When I finally got him in his front door and pointed toward the bedroom of what turned out to be a second-rate apartment in a third-rate part of town, I realized I'd never even been in his domicile before, and I wondered what the fuck the rest of his life was going to be like. His two ex-wives aren't likely to check up on him or even show up for his funeral, and he doesn't have any kids that I know of. Hayes was a one-trick pony. He loved his job. It obviously didn't love him back.

I'm home far too late to wake my beloved, but when I stagger into the living room this morning sometime after ten, I do give her a big hug and a bigger kiss.

"What's that for?" Cindy asks.

For being here, I tell her.

"They'd never do that to you," she says, when I recount the sad last day of Hayes.

"They might."

"Well," she says, "you won't have to worry about coming home to an empty house if it happens."

That, I tell her, is a not inconsequential perk.

"Why do you use five-dollar words all the time?" she asks. "Just say, 'That would be good.'"

I tell her that would indeed be good, if it comes to that.

✦ ✦ ✦

IT'S ALMOST lunchtime when I get the call from Sarah.

"There's a body," she says.

This one is outside the city limits by a good twenty miles, but the modus operandi got Sarah's antenna up when one of the county reporters got word and called it in. So Sarah asked the reporter to inquire about fingers.

"Four missing?" I ask.

"Yep. Everything but the thumb. I don't know why the sheriff's department made us ask about it. Hell, they had to know this was the same maniac, either that or a copycat. It's like they were just not going to mention that little detail."

It is the nature of law enforcement, I remind my boss and former tutee, to hide the facts from the news media.

"Yeah," she says, "I keep forgetting that."

A couple of cyclists found a woman's body in some woods a few feet off the Capital Trail just across the Charles City County line. Her throat was cut.

I'm vaguely familiar with the location. In one of the most ill-advised decisions of my life, I let Cindy talk me into renting a couple of bicycles and venturing onto the trail, which is a good way to get from Richmond to Williamsburg if you don't have a car and can't afford bus fare. The state has built this lovely paved path, fifty-three miles of it, so that cyclists can do something other than clog up vehicular traffic and dent car fenders with their bodies.

The day we went biking, we got as far as the Charles City-Henrico county line before I told Cindy that I'd enjoyed about as much bicycling as I could stand. She said I'd probably have enjoyed it more if I'd not tried to smoke and cycle at the same time.

The body the outdoors enthusiasts found seems to have been there for at least a couple of days, and no identification has been found so far.

A call to the county sheriff's department gets me very little additional information. On a whim, I drive out there. That part of Charles City County is mostly swamp. The crime scene is next to the James River, right across from Turkey Island.

By the time I arrive, the excitement is pretty much over and the body's been removed, but there are still sheriff's department cars parked there. Charles City County probably has about four murders a year, so I guess the cops can be excused for getting a hard-on when they are gifted with one.

Two deputies are having a smoke leaning on their cars next to the crime tape trying to stay warm on a miserable January day. I take a picture of the tape with my iPhone camera, which seems to somehow offend them, but when I whip out a Camel and light up, they sense a kindred spirit and decide not to bust my chops.

One of them, a Black guy, says he's lived around here all his life, across the line in Henrico. When he tells me exactly which community, I ask him if he knows any Lees or Slades. It turns out that he went to school with Richard, my cousin whom I once saved from spending the rest of his life in jail for a crime he didn't commit.

"You're that guy!" the Black cop says. "You're the one that got him off." The white deputy seems less impressed, but my foot's in the door.

"Yeah, I see Richard all the time," he says. "Man, it wasn't right what they did to him."

Richard Slade spent half his adult life in prison, for another crime he did not commit, before justice finally got off her ass and freed him. Then, just as he was getting used to civilian clothes, he got nailed again. After the cops finally realized he was once again innocent, with a little help from the fourth estate, he got to have a life.

Sometimes it does help if your ink-stained wretch didn't just blow into town two days ago. You live here sixty years, you know some folks.

The Black deputy tells me a lot more than maybe the high sheriff would have preferred.

The woman, he says, appeared to be about fifty years old. She was Black too. She didn't have any identification on her. And, yes, she was missing all the digits except her thumb from her right hand.

Her throat was cut, he said, from ear to ear.

"Damn near cut her head off," he says, shaking his head. "Somebody was sore pissed at the lady, seems like."

Did it seem a little weird, I ask, that she had no identification?

"Tell you the truth," the deputy says, "she looked like she'd had some hard times. She was missin' some teeth, and her clothes looked like they were pretty well-worn."

We all three go and sit in the Black guy's squad car. He says he thinks he remembers Artie Lee "but that was a long time ago." The white deputy gives me a look when I tell them that Artie was my father.

"Yeah," the Black guy says. "I can see some resemblance there, now that you mention it."

There isn't much else the deputies know or are willing to impart to a reporter, but I stick around and shoot the shit for a while. Hell, it's pleasant to sit in a car on a cold, sunny day, enjoying what Cindy calls the "windshield factor," and these guys aren't bad company. Even the white guy loosens his sphincter a little after a while.

About fifteen minutes later, as I'm about to head back to the city, a car pulls up, a boat of a Plymouth that looks like it qualifies for antique status.

A heavy-set African American woman who appears to be in her fifties gets out.

She walks over to the car where we're sitting and bangs on the driver's window.

"Where is she?" she asks. She asks it like she wants some answers right damn now.

The Black deputy lowers his window.

"My sister," she says. "I want my sister."

Both the deputies get out of the car now. The woman doesn't seem cowed by uniforms. I get out too.

They finally get her calmed down enough to find out who "she" is and why the woman thinks the deputies know anything about her.

The woman in question, we learn, is Kizzie Long. She is the sister of the woman in the Plymouth, who identifies herself as Shondra Bowles. Kizzie Long disappeared two days ago. When Ms. Bowles heard that a woman's body had been found along the Capital Trail, she says she knew it was her sister.

"What makes you think it was her?" the white deputy asks.

"She told me she was scared," she says. "She said somebody was out to get her. She'd got a postcard, and it scared her. She didn't let me see it, but said it was about old scores bein' settled.

"And then when she went out to walk on that trail day before yesterday, and she didn't come back, I feared the worst."

She said she hadn't called the sheriff's department yet, figuring correctly that the sheriff's department wasn't going to get too exercised about a Black adult female who had only been missing for a day or two.

The deputies are willing to show her a photograph of the body.

She doesn't break down right away, just walks way over to her car and leans against it. Then she starts howling.

"We thought she was safe now that she was home and all," she says when she calms down a little. She doesn't even have a coat on. I guess she left in a hurry when she got the news. I lend her my jacket. She sits there shivering against the car. Finally the deputies coax her back inside. They don't seem to mind that I tag along, or maybe they don't notice.

The deputies want her to come with them to the morgue for positive identification. She says she'll follow them there. She seems unwilling to ride with the deputies, who are understandably worried about her mental state at the moment. I offer to drive her instead.

Before they leave, I ask Shondra Bowles what she meant about her sister being "home and all."

The deputies aren't that thrilled with my butting in, but she waves them off and answers me.

"She got in some trouble when she was younger, got messed up on drugs and stuff," she says. "She's been in and out of prison since she was, I reckon, nineteen. She just got out the last time two months ago. She acted like she was finally ready to walk the straight and narrow."

"Where was she, before they released her?"

I kind of know, but she confirms it.

"The women's prison, up in Goochland County."

The deputies are at least vaguely aware that somebody's been killing Richmond's citizens at a prodigious rate, even by our usual standards. Even out here, I see the occasional newspaper box, and they do have TV and Internet.

To make sure they make the connection, I remind the cops that Maiden Broom, the prime and as yet at-large suspect, was also a guest of the state at the same facility until the last three weeks.

"Holy shit," says the white deputy.

I promise the deputies that I'll drive Ms. Bowles to the morgue, and they finally agree to that.

Shondra Bowles is a mess, having just learned that her sister has been butchered. I don't ask her much on the way to the morgue, just let her wail.

When we're within eyesight of the place, I finally ask her if she knew of anyone who was incarcerated with her sister who might have had a grudge against her.

"There was one woman," Shondra says when she recovers a little. "Last time I visited Kizzie there, she said this white woman was always threatening her. I think she said they got into a fight, something about the white woman trying to jump into the food line ahead of her. But she said that ever since, the white woman always gave her the fish-eye, said she'd get her sooner or later.

"But that wouldn't of been nothin' to kill somebody over."

I agree in principle, but I'm starting to suspect that it doesn't take much to get on Maiden Broom's permanent shit list.

I deliver Shondra Bowles to the morgue. She is agreeable, now that she's calmed down, to letting the deputies take her back to her car later.

Back in town, I stop for a barbecue sandwich at Buzz and Ned's and then head over to police headquarters.

L.D. is, as usual, thrilled to see me. He's even solicitous enough to ask me "what the fuck" I want.

I explain to him what the woman over in Charles City told me.

"They were both in stir together, and they knew each other. The sister said they had some bad blood."

"Well, that's just goddamn great," the chief says. "I guess we'll have to add this one to the list too."

I congratulate L.D. for affording the victim an ounce or so of human kindness.

He glares at me.

"Human kindness ain't going to do shit," he says. "We've got to catch this bitch before she does any more damage."

That would be a good idea, I concur. I ask if there have been any Maiden sightings in Dogtown.

"If there were, you'd be the last to know," he says. "We're combing the city, and nobody has seen her. We even got the damn sketch artist to come up with something, based on the last photo they had of her at Goochland. Not a damn bite, yet."

"Well, I hope she doesn't have any more scores to settle. If I'd ever stepped on this woman's toes, I'd be leery about leaving the house these days."

I ponder what I can write about this. From what I've been told, the victim this time was killed pretty much the same way as the other four. I know that Kizzie Long had a run-in with Maiden Broom when they were locked up.

I can't get the chief to confirm that Maiden is the prime and only suspect in the Charles City killing, but anybody with eyes and a brain will figure that one out when I write it.

"You're going to stir up more shit, aren't you?" L.D. says. He sounds tired. He doesn't try very hard to stop me.

Yeah, I tell him, I'm going to stir up more shit.

Back in the newsroom, I inform Sarah and Wheelie that the killing along the Capital Trail probably is tied to the four murders currently roiling the Holy City.

They agree with me that sentient beings would conclude there's a connection here, and that we should inform our readers of this as soon as possible. The "no comment" from L.D. pretty much confirms that we now have five murders linked by a common thread, that thread probably being Maiden Broom.

✦ ✦ ✦

THE STORY goes online by seven thirty, just late enough, I figure, that the TV folk will have to wait until the late news to poach it from us. Except, as Sarah reminds me, they have websites too. Fifteen minutes after we break the story of Kizzie Long's death and the probable connection to the earlier murders, it's on all four local stations' sites. Only two of the four credit the paper for breaking the story.

"Is there even any such thing as a scoop anymore?" I ask Sarah, who tells me we do the same thing to TV when they break something first.

Except, I remind her, they almost never do break anything first, just wait for us hopeless dinosaurs with our printing presses to do their work for them.

"There is that," Sarah concedes.

The mayor, always ready with a quote, says that city and county law enforcement are on the case. Between the lines, he tries to convey that he's frustrated it's taking so long to track down "this monster," hoping our readers will forget that he was adamant for days that the killer was already locked up.

There's a sidebar, too, on the fact that Sylvester Simms's grieving brother has filed a lawsuit seeking a few million from the city. His mouthpiece, of course, is Marcus Green.

Whoever wins or loses in the great roulette wheel of life, Marcus's number always comes up. Somebody's always screwing somebody, and my ambulance-chasing acquaintance is forever there to get his slice of justice when and if it's finally meted out.

And I'm continuing to nip at the mayor's heels. That story tomorrow will go out of its way to remind readers that Our Leader might be at least partially responsible for a murderer still among us, in addition to being the reason Sly Simms's scum-sucking sibling is likely to win the lawsuit lottery sometime soon.

Meanwhile the corrections folks keep trying to come up with a valid excuse for letting Maiden Broom out of prison early, or at all. Leighton's on that one like MSG at a Chinese buffet.

✦ ✦ ✦

Logic is not rampant in twenty-first-century print journalism. At a time when I'm neck deep in the only story anybody in Richmond seems to care about these days, I find out I'm being furloughed.

The Grimm Group does this to us from time to time, when the numbers don't look good—and they seldom do.

After I've filed my third story for tomorrow's edition, Wheelie calls me into his office.

"Who's going to cover this shit?" I ask, not quietly, when I'm told that I'll be taking the next seven days off without pay. I do vaguely recall being told a few months ago that we all had to endure a no-paycheck week sometime in the next six months.

"And your six months are up this week," Wheelie explains.

He says he'll put Chuck Apple on the Maiden Broom beat, in addition to covering night cops for me.

"And maybe Leighton can help out some. I mean, she's kind of got her foot in the door there anyhow."

Yeah, I'm thinking, and she'd love to get her entire comely young body in there and fatten her résumé at my expense.

I feel for Wheelie. He and Sarah always get to deliver the bad news. If we win some of those cheap-ass press association awards or we find out there won't be any layoffs for the next few weeks, you can count on our publisher, Benson Stine, aka BS, to grace us with his rosy cheeks and bespoke suit.

But I can't resist telling Wheelie how much this is complete and utter bullshit. Chuck's a good guy, but he doesn't have my sources, he's covering two other beats, and I've been flogging this story now for more than two weeks.

"Maybe you could give him a few tips, point him in the right direction," Wheelie says. "Besides it's only a week. Then you can get right back on it."

Wheelie and I both know that's crap. Unless Maiden Broom mercifully disappears from our fair city, this thing's got to come to a head in the next few days. I mean, how hard can it be to find one fifty-year-old white woman in Dogtown?

But Wheelie's got a wife and kids, and like the rest of us, his chances of landing somewhere else at a similar salary get slimmer by the year. He's got to take whatever crap our corporate masters dish out, pass it down to the rest of us, and act like he likes it.

I tell Wheelie that I'll keep my sources to myself, and that maybe I'll do a little pro bono on this one.

He lowers his voice a little or looks around like he's afraid the publisher might be somehow listening in.

"You know that's just what they'd like you to do, right?"

I nod. Yeah, I'm playing right into the bean-counters' greasy paws. I'm a news addict. So shoot me.

✦ ✦ ✦

IF MY job were a football game, somebody should be whistled for piling on.

After filing three stories and hoping for a crime-free night on the police beat, I'm instead graced with the worst confluence of bad and stupid that's happened on my watch lately.

At least there seems to be some kind of twisted logic in the five murders in the Dogtown Slasher spree. Crazy person decides to get even with everybody who's ever looked at her sideways.

What happened tonight takes "meaningless" to a whole 'nother level.

A family driving home from a birthday celebration had its car sprayed with what appeared to be at least thirty bullets. A mother and one of the kids, a two-year-old, are dead. It happened on Hull Street, just west of the city line. The morons who did it were caught within forty-five minutes.

It's all over before I hear about it. I'm tipped off on the q.t. by Peachy Love. She says I'll have to confirm it through either the city or county cops. She tells me, off the record, that the shooters hit the wrong car. Four of the five of them were under sixteen.

"One of 'em," she says, "and he couldn't have been more than fourteen years old, according to the cop that I talked with, seemed to think, no harm, no foul, since they didn't mean to shoot at the people they killed."

I hear Peachy sigh.

"Hell of a world to be raising children in," says the woman who has recently taken on an orphaned infant.

It takes me an hour to confirm the basics of the senseless double homi, file my fourth bylined story of the day, and go home to drown myself in bourbon.

Cindy's waiting up for me.

When I tell her of my current furloughed status as I'm watering down my first Early Times of the evening, she starts making plans for a romantic getaway.

When I tell her that I can't do that, not as long as we've got a serial killer stalking Richmond, she asks me if I've lost my mind.

"You know you're just giving them what they want," she says. "Why pay you when they know you'll work for free?"

I tell her I've already heard that song once tonight.

CHAPTER SIXTEEN

Thursday, January 21

WHEN I check my cell phone sometime after nine, I see that I have a missed call. The number doesn't look familiar. I figure it's from somebody collecting money for cops or orphans or some such shit. Maybe I should start a charity for furloughed journalists.

Still it appears to be a local number, so I click the little arrow and give a listen.

Pretty soon, I'm sure the caller isn't trying to relieve me of my dwindling savings. More like offering trouble, free of charge.

With no preamble, she cuts to the chase.

"Keep your goddamn nose out of my business," a hoarse, raspy voice says. "I know where you live. I know where Andi lives too." Then she recites Andi and Walter's address.

The message ends.

"Who was that?" Cindy asks across the breakfast table.

Not a friend, I reply.

When I explain further, she gets somewhat agitated. I try to calm her by telling her that I get threats all the time.

This one, though, does have me a little spooked. I've never heard Maiden Broom's voice, but I'd feel pretty safe right now betting that was her.

"You need to call Andi," Cindy says.

The idea of having my family dragged into this really pisses me off. It scares me a little too.

I phone my daughter. She's at home today, trying to help a six-year-old get an education via Zoom or whatever the hell they're using in COVID world.

"And they know where we live?" Andi asks. Part of me regrets telling her anything, but having bad stuff happen to my only offspring because I didn't want to worry her is not a thing I could live with.

I tell her that I'm sure it's just an idle threat, and that the woman I suspect of making the call is on the run and in no position to go on the offensive.

"Hey, Dad," Andi says. "I read the papers. I know they found another body out in Charles City County."

She says she's going to call Walter at work, then pack up my grandson and go over to my mother's.

"She doesn't know where Grandma Peggy lives, does she?"

I tell her I'm sure she doesn't, not being at all sure as I say it.

I know Andi doesn't blame me for bringing trouble to her doorstep, but there is a hint of irritation mixed in with the anxiety.

"We'll get this straightened out," I promise her before she hangs up.

L.D. Jones doesn't blow me off when I tell him about the call I got. He promises to have a cop car make a run through the Fan neighborhood where Andi and Walter live every hour or so. Hell, that's about all he can do, other than find this lunatic.

It doesn't take long to determine that the call came from a burner phone, no doubt long since discarded.

With nothing to do except chase a story, unhindered by the tiresome weight of a paycheck, I spring into action. Well, shuffle into it, anyhow.

I remind Cindy that The Voice also said she knew where I live, which means she knows where Cindy lives too.

"Hell," my beloved says, "let her bring it on. Let her meet my little friend."

Yes, Cindy is armed and even more dangerous than usual. Maybe it's part of her redneck Oregon Hill upbringing, but she's a pistol-packing momma now. I'm a little uneasy, but she's let her brother teach her the basics of gun safety.

"Maybe you'll save me," I say.

"After I save myself," she replies. "If I have time."

I call Leighton Byrd, who's still on the parole board story like fleas on a hound.

"What was that guy's name, the one who picked up Maiden when they released her?"

"James Caldwell," she says. "And I've already checked. Nobody by that name shows up in the city. And it could be a pseudonym. Last night, I finally got up with the guy from the parole board who signed her out, and he didn't give me the sense that they checked this James Caldwell's ID that thoroughly."

I ask her how she was able to get in contact with anyone at the board, which is kind of avoiding the news media these days as they scramble to cover their very-exposed asses.

"I have my ways," she says. Then she asks me to hold on while she checks her notes.

"There was one other thing," she says when she comes back. "I asked the guy if he could describe him. He was pretty average-looking. White guy, gray-brown hair, little over six feet tall, a tad overweight. And one other thing: he had either a birthmark or some kind of burn."

"Where?"

"On his neck. The guy said it was on the right side, just above his shirt collar. Said it looked like a cantaloupe."

"A cantaloupe?"

"Not as big as a cantaloupe, but shaped and colored like one. You know, kind of tan and green."

I ask her if she's passed that tidbit on to the cops.

"Haven't even put it in print yet," she says.

I thank her for the information and tell her that I might have something interesting to add to James Caldwell's profile after I make a call.

"Like what?"

"Like maybe his real name."

I won't tell her more, but I promise that, if my hunch is correct, she'll get half a double byline.

"Can I be on top this time?" she asks.

Don't talk dirty, I reply.

I stop by Peggy's to gently urge her and Awesome to be wary of strangers, explaining the call I got.

"Yeah, Andi already called," my mom says. "She's coming over with William in a while. Why are you always getting in some kind of shit or other?"

Occupational hazard, I explain. She says not to worry, that she and the Dude can take care of themselves.

✦ ✦ ✦

It's my intention to call the chief back with a hot tip, but I need to talk to Carson Broom first.

After a few rings, the old geezer answers his phone.

"What?" he says in a less-than-welcoming tone.

I reintroduce myself.

"I need to ask you something."

He says he's busy. I tell him it won't take long, and it might help the cops find his niece.

"When Buddy Broom disappeared . . ." I begin.

"Who?"

I'm starting to worry a little about Carson's cognitive issues. I jog his memory about his long-lost nephew.

On the same page at last, I ask him if Buddy Broom had any marks on him, anything that might make him identifiable.

"Jesus Christ," Carson says, "we're talking, what, thirty-four damn years ago? I've forgot what the son of a bitch looked like."

I encourage him to think hard.

Finally I get a response.

"There was one thing, now that you mention it. He had an accident when he was a teenager, fell against a hot stove, I think. Left a scar."

"Where?"

"On his neck. It had healed up OK by the time he disappeared, but it was kind of an ugly thing. He'd wear turtlenecks to school, even in warm weather, to hide it."

"Did it look like a cantaloupe?"

"A what? A cantaloupe? Hell, I don't know. I guess it might have, now that you mention it. How'd you know that?"

Just a lucky guess, I tell him.

✦ ✦ ✦

I CALL L.D. and tell him who I'm pretty sure picked up Maiden Broom when she was released from the women's pen.

"But he probably isn't going by James Caldwell, or at least there's nobody by that name showing up in any city directory."

I also tell him about the mark on his neck.

"A fucking cantaloupe?"

"That's what I'm told."

He wants me to sit on this until his mighty force can spring into action.

"Not a chance, L.D."

He accuses me of interfering with a police investigation.

"How the fuck are we going to find him if he knows we know who he is now?"

I tell him that he's lucky I called him at all, didn't just put it on the website and let him find out about it like everybody else.

"You know what he looks like now," I add, "down to his damn scar. And you wouldn't have any of that without me. Hell, I thought you'd be grateful."

He doesn't sound grateful as he hangs up.

I give Leighton a call.

"Her brother? Her goddamn brother? Why didn't I figure that out myself?"

I assure her that she would have eventually. Then I go old school and dictate what I think I've learned about James Caldwell's true identity so she can add it to what she's written already.

"This is how you all used to do it, back in the Stone Age?" she asks when I start telling her about rewrite men and life before the Internet.

"Man," she says when I'm done, "the guy's been missing for thirty-some years. This is going to sell some papers."

Or, I suggest, they'll all just read it online and then watch while the TV stations steal it and run with it.

"Whatever," Leighton says. "We both know who got the goods, right?"

Now, I tell her, it'd be really good if the cops were able to find their ass with both hands before Maiden Broom kills again. I tell her about my phone message this morning.

"Damn, Willie," she says, "she's really going to go around the bend when she finds out about this."

I note that I kind of know that and am hoping that the chief's troops get off the schneid and find Buddy Broom and his demented sister very soon.

"Are you really doing this on your own time?"

I confirm that I am indeed enjoying a payless furlough.

"You ought to just tell them to go fuck themselves," she suggests.

"And miss all this fun? You'd do the same thing."

"Yeah," she says after a short pause. "You're right. I'm an idiot too."

"Don't forget my byline," I remind my ambitious colleague.

"Right underneath mine," she replies.

✦ ✦ ✦

I MAKE sure that Sarah and Wheelie both know the latest. They each express their gratitude over my freebie, although neither of them offers to march up to BS's office and demand that my furlough be rescinded.

"Have you heard the latest about Weather Guy?" Sarah asks.

Poor Weather Guy. Guy Flowers, who draws a pretty sizable paycheck for doing in print what the TV meteorologists do on air, has more dog trouble.

After the two hounds he "adopted" fell in love on camera during one of his online video bits, he gave up on the idea and took them back to the friend from whom he had borrowed them. A neighbor of that friend thought that was newsworthy enough that she called one of the local TV stations and told them about Weather Guy's fickle behavior. Maybe the neighbor just hates newspapers. Lot of that going around.

The station, whose weatherman has been boosting his ratings for years with his own telegenic pooch, was more than delighted to run with it like a beagle chasing a rabbit. On its next evening newscast, there was a photo of the two pups, back home after their star turn.

"It appears," the TV weatherman said, barely stifling a chuckle, "that, despite reports to the contrary, local print journalism is not going to the dogs."

Weather Guy, who has been allowed to continue his video presence, would not have been more reviled if he'd adopted some kid and then left him on the door of the orphanage. His friend caught a pretty good ration, too, after revealing that he'd had the pups altered so that they would not be prone to doing it doggie style, or any other way, again.

"We're not going to fire Weather Guy," Sarah says, "but I told him that if I ever see a dog even cross the set in the background while he's doing his video bit, I'm taking him to a shelter and dropping him off."

I suggest that perhaps Weather Guy should try using a cat. I even volunteer Butterball.

"Congratulations, Willie," she says. "Just when I think things couldn't be worse, you find a way to make it happen."

✦ ✦ ✦

So we now have a pretty good idea what Maiden Broom looks like. In addition, we have an even better description of her brother. The double-byline story includes everything we know so far: the likelihood that they are or have been in the vicinity of O'Toole's in Dogtown, the dubious way the suspect was released from custody compliments of the parole board, the chronology of Maiden's wave of terror so far, plus, of course, a reminder that somebody has lopped off at least ten fingers from the dead or dying. Handley Pace in design has even come up with updated artist's renderings of how the siblings might look now, based on old photos of Maiden and what the parole board source told Leighton. I'm not sure the caricatures are very helpful, but they seem marginally better than the ones the police have produced. Buddy reminds me a little of a middle-aged Charlie Manson, but, hell, maybe that's what he looks like.

Much of what Leighton and I put together for tomorrow's paper and today's online readers has been told before, but who reads the paper every day?

In the twentieth century, we might have had to cut the story down to maybe 800 words and eschew writing what we've written already. These days, with reporters shrinking even faster than newsprint, there's space aplenty. Used to be, reporters shaved the chaff from their deathless prose so that the last five inches or so didn't wind up on the composing room floor. Now there's no composing room and no limit on verbiage. And the Internet is bottomless.

Sally Velez probably summed it up best when one of our younger reporters asked her yesterday how much she wanted him to write on a city council meeting.

"Write your ass off," Sally advised. And so they do.

I contribute a sidebar in which I talk to some of the victims' survivors. We're always told that we spend much more time on the perps than we do their prey, so I make a couple of calls.

Harlan Bell's widow wants nothing to do with me. She's living alone and petrified that "that monster" is coming back for her. I try to reassure her on that note, but I understand her fear.

Kevin McCaskill is still trying to get his head around the fact that his parents were butchered for no better reason than the fact that they told the truth about what they saw and heard all those years ago.

Lemuel Cartwright's cousin said he couldn't understand why the killer was still loose.

And Chip Pratt says his daughter's started having nightmares and is probably going to be seeing a shrink soon.

✦ ✦ ✦

Iт's а nice, two-Camel walk over to Peggy's in Oregon Hill on a decent January afternoon, sweater weather. Cindy, who is done Zooming with her students for the day, comes with me.

Andi and young William are already there. Andi seems to have gotten over her unease about the recent rantings of Maiden Broom and says they'll go back home when Walter gets off work.

"They'll probably have caught the bad lady by then anyhow," she reassures my grandson, who is playing a game of checkers with Awesome Dude and apparently winning.

I apologize to all for inadvertently getting them caught up in a crime spree that should have nothing at all to do with them.

"Aw, don't worry about it," Peggy says. She seems a little edgy, though, maybe because she isn't stoned, showing at least minimal consideration for her impressionable grandson. "Hell, everybody on the Hill's armed all the time anyhow. Bitch better not come over here."

I'm not sure Peggy's right about that. Maybe forty years ago that would have been the case, but I'd have thought gentrification would have lowered the firearms-per-human numbers a bit.

"If you need one," Cindy says, lowering her voice so William doesn't hear, "I can get you one." Then she shows Andi the piece she's carrying in her purse.

"My protector," I murmur.

CHAPTER SEVENTEEN

Friday, January 22

YESTERDAY ENDED with some good news. Peggy is getting her shot. It has been determined by the gods of public health that her status as a seventy-eight-year-old with marijuana lungs makes her eligible for a free poke from Pfizer.

She got the call last night, and they want her to come over this morning at nine.

So I'm out of the house by eight. I pick her up and take Awesome along for the ride. Walter's taking off work today, so I'm hoping he has my daughter and grandson somewhere safe.

Awesome and I have to wait in the damn parking deck, pandemic restrictions being what they are. We're sitting there, me smoking and Awesome boring the shit out of me telling me about some no-talent competition he and my mother saw on one of the cable channels last night.

My phone buzzes.

"If you come over here now," Peggy says, "they say they can take care of you and Awesome."

It's crazy. For the last two weeks, sane people in Richmond, meaning the ones who aren't COVID deniers, have been scrambling around for a shot, following rumors and dead ends, driving to towns half a state away, and now suddenly, just like that, here is our salvation.

We hustle over to the clinic. Forty-five minutes later, we're all vaccinated. Evidently the hospital had more doses than patients. They even lined us up for the second shot in three weeks.

"Too bad Cindy didn't come with you," Peggy says.

Yeah, when she finds out what she missed, I'm thinking she might want to give me a shot. Pissed with a pistol. My survivor guilt doesn't last long though.

I drop off Peggy and Awesome and head back to the Prestwould.

When I get there, there's a big kerfuffle in the lobby. Not unexpectedly, Feldman is the cause.

It turns out that our happy condo community's resident McGrumpy still doesn't believe in COVID. He is, as I enter the door, not wearing a mask and is on the verge of getting the shit beat out of his aged ass by Pete Garland.

Pete and his wife, Patti, our neighbors across the hall, have been quarantining for the last several days after testing positive. Patti, Pete tells me, is having a rough time with it. He's wondering if he needs to take her to the hospital.

"And this son of a bitch," Pete says, pointing at McGrumpy, "won't even wear a goddamn mask."

"It's all a hoax," Feldman says, his lip poked out.

This understandably sets off the man whose wife could be pushing up daisies soon due to this "hoax."

Fred Baron is holding Pete Garland back, which is probably a good thing. Not that Feldman doesn't need killing, but Pete's too good a man to go to prison for manslaughter.

The condo board doesn't seem to know what to do about masks, other than appeal to the residents' good nature. In most cases, this works. But then there's always a Feldman in any decent-sized condo building.

I want to hit the son of a bitch myself. Marcia the manager has called Custalow to intervene, and finally peace is restored. Feldman is told that he's not allowed to ride the elevator unless he's masked, and that he will be forcibly removed if he tries to get on without one. Since he lives on the tenth floor, that should be inducement enough, but the stubborn bastard probably will walk up and down nine flights of stairs just to be a dick.

He threatens to sue the Prestwould, and all of us, for violating his rights. When he tries to get on the elevator, Abe puts one of his big paws on his shoulder and squeezes a little.

"Mr. Feldman," he says, "if you get on that elevator, I will have to take steps to stop you."

McGrumpy starts squawking about "that big Indian" assaulting him. We all assure him that none of us saw a thing or intend to see anything else Custalow might or might not do. Seeing that he's on his own, Feldman harrumphs and heads for the stairs.

"Nine-floor climb will probably kill him," Pete says.

"No such luck," Marcia the manager adds, then begs us not to quote her.

I give Cindy the blow-by-blow of *l'affaire* Feldman. Then I casually mention that the good people at the VCU hospital were able to squeeze Awesome and me in.

This does not go over well, as expected.

"Why didn't you call me?" she sputters. "I could have been there in ten minutes."

I try to explain that they were pretty adamant about the timing, and that she chose not to come with me to the hospital. She points out that she had to conduct a Zoom class at ten.

"Damn, damn, damn," she says, banging her fist on the coffee table loudly enough to scare the cats. "You and some guy who has nothing to do all day but get stoned can just waltz right in. I, on the other hand, a dedicated public schoolteacher, am still out in the cold."

There isn't much else I can say that's going to make this better. I really would have given my shot to Cindy if I'd had the option. When she calms down, I think she'll know that.

For the time being, though, the thing I need to make myself is scarce.

✦ ✦ ✦

I'M ON my way in the direction of O'Toole's when my phone wakes up in my pocket. The state now says talking on the phone while driving is as distracting as a blow job. To avoid the prospect of a ticket, I pull over to an empty space on Broad Street and fish out the cell before the first bars of "I Heard It Through the Grapevine" stop repeating.

"How you all comin' with that Dogtown Slasher shit?" Big Boy Sunday inquires, forgoing a more conventional greeting.

Big Boy is in his car, no doubt being chauffeured around his little drug kingdom by one of his young felonious interns.

The big man is not what anyone would call a pillar of the Black community, although he might give more to charity than your average Episcopalian businessman. What he is, to me, is a source. He knows what's going on. He has eyes and ears in places the cops and your diligent news reporter don't even know exist.

And so, when Big Boy calls, I answer.

I tell him that I've put everything I know in this morning's paper.

"Thass nice," he says. "Good information, about that scar and all. Maybe the cops can find their asses with both hands now and wrap that nutcase and her brother up. It's gettin' so it ain't even safe to be on the streets anymore. They're even killing Black folks."

I wisely choose not to mention that a large portion of the bodies that show up at the city morgue probably were either Big Boy's employees or his rivals. The joke around some parts of the city is that he shows up at a funeral, gives the deceased's momma or girlfriend an envelope stuffed with cash, with everybody knowing the poor sap residing in a pine box got put there by the big man's henchmen.

I ask Big Boy if he has any insight into the case, something that might have eluded less-observant individuals.

He laughs.

"Yeah, observant. That's me. Observant as a motherfucker."

He takes his time, probably so he can fully savor whatever he's eating. I wonder if Big Boy has a kitchen in his house. Every time we talk, he's riding and eating.

"I might have something," he says. "I s'pose I could give this to the cops, but me and them aren't on that solid a footing, you know what I mean? And you've been good to me. So here it is."

What Big Boy knows is worth the wait.

"There's a house over there near Reedy Creek," he says. "One of my associates owns the place next door."

He says the house hasn't been rented for at least the past six months, but the owner hangs on to it, "hopin' for better days so he can sell the thing."

What Big Boy's associate noticed was that somebody seemed to be squatting on the property.

"He said the place is surrounded by a big old wooden fence, so you can't even see the house, but that it backs up to an alley, and he saw a car come out of there into that alley two days ago. He didn't get a good look, but he said he was pretty sure there was a white woman driving. Said it seemed suspicious."

Big Boy's informant didn't know what kind of car it was, other than that it was white.

Why, I ask, didn't somebody call the police?

Big Boy laughs.

"Nobody really wants the po-po around, you know. Gets in the way of business.

"But with all the shit that's been going on lately, it just seemed like it was my civic duty to let somebody know. Just in case this has anything to do with what you're looking for."

Big Boy gives me the address and describes the house. I realize I drove right by it on my snooping mission. I ask him if the owner had gone around to check on the interlopers on his property.

"He might not even know about it. Evidently he doesn't check on the place too much. And I thought it might be safer if somebody else took a look."

I hear Big Boy laugh.

"Somebody that don't mind gettin' shot at."

My informant belches and continues.

"So anyhow, you can get our fine police force on this if you want. Better to come from you than from me. Hell, somebody's got to stop this foolishness."

I thank Big Boy for his civic-mindedness.

"Who knows?" he says. "I might need somethin' from you some day."

When and if that day comes, I hope the "somethin'" doesn't involve a major felony. Big Boy is scrupulous about collecting on old debts.

✦ ✦ ✦

BEFORE I call the chief with the big news, I decide to see for myself.

I'm not that far from Dogtown. I cross the Nickel Bridge, then drive east on Forest Hill, take a right a couple of blocks down from O'Toole's, and a couple of turns later, there it is.

Like Big Boy said, you can't see the house for the fence out front, which is smothered in kudzu. But if you turn down the side street, there's that alley he told me about.

I drive down the alley, and there are enough broken slats in the fence that I can get a glimpse of the mystery house. The place is a brick rancher in need of a new roof. What wood there is seems to be halfway to rotted out. There's no garage, just a carport, with a short driveway leading onto the alley.

And in that carport is a white Toyota Corolla.

I drive past the house. Halfway down the alley I stop.

I sit there for twenty minutes, smoking and waiting. Nobody comes in or out.

I call the chief and tell him what I've learned.

"What the hell are you doing conversing with that son of a bitch?" L.D. asks. It is a burr in the chief's butt that he has never been able to nail Big Boy Sunday.

"I didn't call him," I explain. "He called me. The important thing is, this is a pretty good lead, don't you think?"

He has to concede that it is.

"And you went over there by yourself, playing junior detective or some such shit?"

"Senior detective, but that's beside the point. The question is, are you going to do anything about it?"

He tells me he'll decide how to run his police department.

"Hell, I heard they've laid your ass off. What are you doing out working anyhow?"

I explain the difference between layoffs and furloughs. The chief chuckles.

"You just can't leave it alone, can you? Bad as a damn opioid addict."

I tell him somebody's got to find the bad guys and girls, since the police haven't had much luck so far.

He curses me and hangs up.

I go back to O'Toole's and kill an hour. I order the liver and onions with mac and cheese, my favorite vegetable, washed down with a couple of Miller Lites. Nobody I talk with has seen further sign of anyone resembling Maiden Broom.

"Kind of got us spooked," the manager says. It turns out that having the public know a suspected psychopath frequents your establishment isn't all that good for business.

We both assume that the Brooms are getting their provisions from elsewhere now that their connection with O'Toole's has been published in the paper.

I see that our artist's half-assed renderings of Maiden and Buddy are on the wall behind the bar.

I call Cindy to tell her where I am. She's still pissed about missing her big vaccine opportunity, but she allows that she'd be a little more understanding if I were to bring an order of chicken Parmesan home with me.

So I place an order to go, have a third beer, and then make another run over to that brick house. This time I park down the side street, a block beyond the alley. I can see anybody coming or going from here. The plan is to hang around for a few more minutes, just in case.

Fifteen minutes later, I see an unmarked cop car roll by. The car circles the block and then stops a block and a half away, behind me. I drive off and loop back so I come up behind the cops. I can see that one of them is Gillespie. When I beep my horn, he jumps and then gets out, looking as if he'd like to commit a little police brutality.

He sees it's me, so he puts the Taser away.

"What the fuck are you doin' here, Black?" he asks. "You're interfering with police work."

"Who do you think told the chief where to look?"

"That don't mean shit," he says. "You need to move your ass out of here now."

I tell him I have to get home anyhow, and open the Styrofoam container to give him a whiff of the chicken Parm. He looks envious.

He looks toward the fence-hidden house.

"You think they're in there?" he asks.

I shrug my shoulders.

"Somebody said there's squatters in there, and they saw a white woman leave once in the middle of the night. Not a lot of white folks around here."

He is willing to tell me that the police are going to stake the place out and see who goes in or out. A search warrant is in the offing, too, but I can tell that the cops aren't all that eager to go rushing in just yet, considering Maiden Broom's apparent proclivity for mayhem.

"Think she's armed, I mean other than the knife?" he asks me. "And then there's the brother. I mean, he's probably in there, too, right? Fucker looks like Charlie Manson."

Could be, I concede. All we know about Buddy Broom so far is that he was apparently the one who picked up his sister when she was released.

On the way back with Cindy's cheesy delight, I text Peachy Love and ask her to call me if she can manage it.

She phones back within a minute.

"Taking the day off to look after Aurora," she says. She and Ronald have been playing tag team, and he's out of town on business today.

She already knows, though, what I told the chief.

"We're going to do this one very carefully," she tells me. "We'd like to do it without a body count."

I ask her to please call me, day or night, when it looks like something's going to happen.

"Might not be today," she says. "Let Mamma finish her phone call, Sweetie. Let go of Mamma's hair. Sorry, Willie. I've got to go. But I'll keep you posted."

And then, driving home, I think to myself, bullshit. I'm going to be here for this one.

I deliver the goods to Cindy and then explain that I'm headed out again, and that I don't know how long I'll be gone. I give her the details and tell her not to let any strangers in.

She says that, from what two of my ex-wives have told her, a Willie story about eavesdropping on a police stake-out might have been an excuse for an extramarital date.

"But you're older and smarter now," she says, giving me a kiss and telling me to be careful.

Older anyhow.

CHAPTER EIGHTEEN

Saturday, January 23

NOW I remember how much I hate camping.

I did it once with R.P. and Andy, decades ago, at some place up on Skyline Drive. It seemed like a good idea. Beer, steaks, a grill. What could go wrong?

We went up there on a beautiful April day, probably seventy degrees outside. But then the sun went down, and I realized how a drop of twenty degrees felt like a blue norther to someone used to the comforts of climate control. Plus Andy forgot the charcoal lighter.

Last night was sort of like that, substituting the aged Honda for the sleeping bag.

It wasn't a particularly cold night for winter in these parts, but it got below freezing, and insulation is not one of the Accord's strong points.

I had gotten back to Dogtown about five, just before sunset. I brought along a couple of barbecue sandwiches and some hush puppies from Buzz and Ned's and a six-pack to keep me company.

I called Sarah and told her how her intrepid reporter was spending his furlough day.

"I can't believe you're doing that," she said. "You're going to freeze or get your ass shot. Want me to send a photographer up there?"

"To photograph me getting my ass shot?"

I told her it was probably better to limit the news media presence to one car. I was expecting somebody with a uniform to try to roust me as soon as they figured out who was in the civilian car.

"Well," she said, "call me when something happens."

The place I chose was half a block back from the closest unmarked cop car. I recognized half a dozen of them and figured there were more. It was quiet, probably quieter than usual, because any sentient human being had to know something was up. Unmarked police cars are amazingly easy to spot.

Not long after sunset, I realized that I needed a bigger coat. Every hour or so, I'd turn on the engine and heat things up, but as soon as I shut it down, the cold came creeping in again.

The cops knew I was there. Hell, L.D. himself came over sometime around ten to suggest that I get the hell out and quit interfering with police work.

I told him I wasn't interfering with anything.

"You're loitering," he replied.

"Goddammit, L.D.," I said, "you'd still be chasing your tail on this one if I hadn't tipped you off. If I want to sit here and freeze my butt off waiting for you to do whatever the fuck it is you all are intending to do, it's my business."

"Well," the chief said, conceding that I had a horse in this race, "you should've brought along a thermos of coffee instead of a fuckin' six-pack. And I better not catch you driving drunk either."

So he left me alone. He didn't even have me arrested for public exposure when I slipped down one of the alleys to relieve myself of those Millers.

I called Cindy a couple of times, but after eleven, it was just me and my Honda. I thought about driving back home for coffee and a blanket, but I didn't know when the fireworks might start, so I hunkered down and waited out the night.

✦ ✦ ✦

I DID manage to doze off at some point, because L.D. rousts me by banging on the window. It's almost seven A.M. The sky is getting light in the east.

"If you can wake your ass up," he says, "the show's about to start. Just stay out of the fuckin' way."

I'm reminded of the last time Richmond's finest woke me up at first light. That time, it was to free me from a hostage situation brought on by my near-lethal nosiness. I have to give the cops credit: They saved my butt even if they did leave me with my abductor's brains staining my shirt and face.

My expectations of a kinder, gentler resolution to this episode are somewhat low. If the doctors' creed is "first, do no harm," I sometimes wonder if the cops aren't more into "first, harm the son of a bitch enough that he doesn't harm us."

It seems cruel to call my editors before sunrise. I check my cell phone, which might be the only camera that has any chance of capturing what's going to happen next.

The "show" starts just as the sun breaks the surface.

The cops move in close, just outside the kudzu fence. The one with the bullhorn tells Maiden Broom and Beverley Broom to come out peacefully, adding that they are surrounded. For several minutes, as the demand is repeated twice, nothing happens.

Then I hear a man's voice coming from somewhere inside the house.

"We ain't coming out," the voice says. "We've got some demands."

I've moved closer to the action. The cops are still behind the fence. They're so focused on the house that they don't seem to notice me. Several of them have big-ass guns aimed at what seems like the only entrance to the property.

"We've got a kid in here," the voice says. "She's kind of scared, and if you don't back the fuck off, we're going to cut her up."

L.D. takes over the bullhorn.

"What do you want?" he says. "How can we help you?"

Like he's a customer service guy for Verizon or something.

And then he makes his request.

"I want to talk to Willie Black."

The chief says it might take a few minutes to find me.

"Bullshit," the voice says. "He's right there with you. Do you think I'm an idiot?"

L.D. is quick to assure the voice, which has to belong to Buddy Broom, that he is second to none in his respect for his intellect.

"Give me a couple of minutes," he says.

"I'll give you five," the voice says. "After that, the kid's gone."

The chief wants to know how the hell the guy inside knows I'm already on the scene. I'm as mystified as he is, although he doesn't believe that.

"I can't let you go in there," he says. I tell him I'm not crazy about the idea, either, but we don't seem to have much choice. Buddy Broom seems to be holding all the cards right now.

"How's it going to look," he asks, "if I let you go in there and they kill your ass?"

I'm sure L.D.'s tender concerns for my well-being are secondary to his fear over how it'll look if he and his minions get a hard-working though unpaid scribe murdered.

While he's mulling his options, he asks Buddy if he can speak to his sister or their hostage.

"You don't need to speak to nobody but me," Buddy Broom replies. "And the clock's ticking."

The chief and a couple of cops who look like they've been to a rodeo or two confer. They consider using flash-bangs and/or smoke grenades and trying to charge the place, but in the end, they agree that sending old Willie in there will buy them some time at least.

L.D. tells Buddy that if they don't hear from me every ten minutes, they're coming in, hostage or not. He doesn't say yes or no to that, just tells him to go fuck himself.

With the clock ticking, it's go time.

They want me to wear a bulletproof vest. I convince them of the foolishness of such an idea.

"I'll be right there, L.D. If he wants to kill me, he'll kill me. Not much way a damn vest is going to save me."

I tell him that I intend to take in a tape recorder, completely unhidden, because why would the guy give a fuck whether I'm recording him or not?

The chief says the man already seems pretty pissed off.

"I wonder what the hell he wants," L.D. says.

Maybe, I suggest, he just wants to chat.

"And then what?" the chief asks.

I don't have an answer for that.

✦ ✦ ✦

THE WIND has picked up a little as I open the gate and make my way onto the property. I approach the house like the front yard is mined, which, for all I know, it is. One good way to get rid of a nosy-ass reporter.

When I'm four feet from the door, it opens an inch, and I walk in.

The room I've entered must be the mudroom. The door shuts behind me, and a light, battery-powered, comes on. I see that blackout curtains are shielding us from the outside world, meaning snipers.

I turn and am face-to-face with Buddy Broom.

He's not a big guy, a little shorter than me. He doesn't look a thing like Charlie Manson. So much for artists' renderings. He's a scroungy-looking guy with hair that's still more blond than gray. An overly large schnoz and a perpetual frown wrinkle mar a face that might have been handsome at one time. His mouth is turned down, which looks like its default position. His pupils are black circles. I am reminded of pictures I've seen of US kids in the jungle during our Vietnam adventure. He's got that thousand-yard stare.

And, of course, he has the cantaloupe scar or whatever on his neck.

He's smoking. I ask him if I can too. He hesitates, then shrugs.

"Sure, what the fuck."

He gives me a light, then leads me into the den and pushes me into a chair. He grabs another one, which he pulls a few feet in front of me, and sits. He's carrying a big honkin'gun. At least it isn't a knife.

He checks to see if I'm wired up.

When I show him the tape recorder, he shrugs.

"Sure," he says, "knock yourself out. That way at least you won't misquote me."

He gets to the point.

"So you're the asshole that's been stirring up so much shit," he says when he's done. "Been wanting to meet you."

He doesn't say it with a lot of warmth.

If I told him the pleasure was all mine, he'd know I was lying.

I ask him where his sister is. After eighteen days on her trail, I feel I'm entitled to see the genuine article at last.

He tells me not to worry about it, that she's in the back with their hostage.

How, I ask him, did you know I was out there?

Buddy smiles, showing a dental portfolio that further detracts from his appearance. It is not a smile that puts one at ease.

"You were seen," is all he says.

He waves his arms, including the one with the presumably loaded gun.

"That's neither here nor there," he says. "I asked you in here because I want to tell you a story."

CHAPTER NINETEEN

THE PLACE is cold as a witch's tit, almost as cold as the Honda was last night. Obviously nobody's been paying the electric bills on this joint. The gas must still be on, though, because I'm getting a hint of it from elsewhere in the house.

Buddy Broom tells me to call the cops and let them know I'm OK, and that I'll stay that way as long as nobody does something stupid. L.D. says to stay in touch.

Buddy gets to the point.

"We wanted somebody to know," he says.

"Know what?" I ask.

He moves his chair a little closer.

"To know that actions have consequences."

I wait for more information.

He gives me the short version of what life was like growing up in his parents' house up in the valley.

"Beverley and Connie were hard on me," he says.

No pity party for you, I'm thinking. At least you had two parents.

As he continues, he'll keep referring to them by their given names, never Mom and Dad.

"Everything had to be perfect. Corporal punishment was the default mode when anything wasn't done quite right."

He said his mother was actually worse than his father, apparently a big fan of a large leather belt.

"I'm surprised she didn't wear the damn thing out," he says.

"You know how I got this?" he asks, pulling back his shirt collar to show me the scar on his neck. "I was fourteen, and I actually stood up to her. Told her I wasn't going to let her beat me anymore. She surprised me by not doing anything at the time, just stared at me and then walked off. I figured, one point for me.

"That night, though, she got even."

While Buddy was sleeping, his mother came into his room with a hot iron and gave him a lasting memento of her affection.

"I should have gone to somebody then, but they kind of had me under their thumb. I've read about the Stockholm Syndrome, and maybe that's what it was.

"Plus I didn't want to leave Maiden back there to deal with them both."

Maiden, he says, had it worse than he did.

"I was the 'good kid.' My grades were pretty decent, and they never saw the need to send me off to some private school to 'straighten me out.'"

Maiden, he says, never begged for mercy when they beat her.

"She just looked them in the eye like, 'Is that all you've got?' Maiden was tough."

But there was more than the beatings.

"Beverley started it when she was about thirteen, I think. She told me some of it later, how it was a relief when he would be kind of tender to her rather than in a rage all the time. But he had a very strange way of show-ing tenderness."

He says their mother knew about it.

"This is perverted as hell, I know, but Maiden swore to me that Connie would sometimes sit and watch while he raped her.

"I don't know what their problem was, never did. I've had a lot of time to think about it. I know that there was some insanity in the family, and it didn't help that the two of them were usually dog drunk not long after the sun went down."

He shakes his head.

"They were so good at turning it on and off. Every-body thought they were just the best couple. Gave great parties. I think their friends felt sorry for them for having a fucked-up kid like Maiden. They made up some bullshit story about me falling onto the stove, and I let them get away with it."

He looks at me.

"I really think they hated us. That's the way it felt to us at the time."

He lets me check in with L.D. again. The chief's getting kind of itchy out there, wanting some kind of resolution. I tell him to stay calm. Being in the middle of a gun battle is not high on my to-do list.

"The worst was before she got sent to that last girls' school, the one in West Virginia."

His father told him that he was taking Maiden away for a couple of days "to see a doctor." Neither he nor their mother was willing to shed any more light on it.

"But I knew. Maiden told me when she got back that he said he'd kill her if she reported it, but she and I were tight, like POWs with a common enemy. So she told me what he was doing to her. And she told me that she was pregnant. She was barely sixteen, and I'm sure Beverley told the doctors his slut daughter had gotten herself knocked up by some local boy.

"When they got back, she was kind of beaten down. I thought she had just finally given up, but I hadn't given her enough credit."

The night after they returned from the "doctor's visit," Maiden came to his room.

"She just said it, flat-out. 'We're going to kill them.' She didn't seem hysterical, or even pissed off. She just said it like it was something that had to be done.

"Which, to tell you the truth, was the way I felt too. I mean, I was a year older than her, but she'd always been the only one trying to protect me. I felt like I hadn't done enough for her. Nobody did."

He said they talked about it, but he didn't really think they would go through with it.

"We planned how we could get away with it, and Maiden said we could say somebody broke in while Beverley and Connie were alone. She said we'd figure out some excuse to be out somewhere at the time. She said nobody would think a couple of kids would kill their own parents."

He left the details to Maiden "and I probably shouldn't have done that, because, despite what she said, I don't think she had much of a plan, other than just killing them."

Outside we can hear the cop radios squawking, and I wonder how much longer they're going to wait before they go all Rambo on us.

I need to hear the rest of this story.

Maiden and Buddy were supposed to go to a party. It was Halloween, and they were going to spend the night at the house of a friend of Maiden's. The friend was supposed to swear that they were there all night and then left early the next morning. The girl was from a well-off family, well-off enough and open-minded enough that their daughter had her own entrance, so her parents didn't have to know what they didn't want to know.

Maiden didn't tell the girl why she had to cover for them, but Buddy says Maiden made her swear she wouldn't tell, no matter what.

"I think the girl was a little bit afraid of Maiden." He laughs and rubs his neck. "Hell, she had reason to be.

"By that time, our sainted parents were just happy we weren't around, I think. Plus, after the abortion, I think they knew they had to let Maiden do whatever she damn well pleased."

They knew Beverley and Connie would, reliable as sunset, be well into their cups by seven.

"Maiden thought it'd be a hoot if we came to the house in costume, like little kids trick-or-treating. She had a witch costume and she had me dressed like a vampire."

It was already pitch-black when they returned to the house. They parked the family car a hundred yards away from the gate and walked in.

"We lived out in the country, far enough away that nobody was likely to see us," he says. "Plus we were in costume. Could've been anybody."

I tell him I know the place.

"That's right," Buddy says, nodding. "You got hold of that asshole uncle of ours. Son of a bitch is lucky he's still breathing."

He knew Maiden had a plan, "But I didn't know about the knife."

They rang the doorbell three times before anybody answered.

"We were far enough out in the woods that they didn't expect any trick-or-treaters. I'm sure they had no candy there. Maybe they could give the little tykes mini bottles. When Connie opened the door, I could see that she was surprised. She said something about us being too fuckin' old for Halloween and she tried to slam the door. We could tell that she was blitzed, as expected.

"That's when Maiden stuck her foot in the door. She said, 'Oh, Mommy, you wouldn't deny your darling children a treat, would you?' She tore off that witch's mask and said, 'Well, in that case, I guess we'll just have to play you a trick.'

"Up to that point, I really thought Maiden might just want to scare the shit out of them. I went along, but I was still thinking that we'd never really do it."

He says Maiden pulled out a butcher knife she'd taken from the kitchen.

"Connie saw who it was and had this look like, 'How dare you mess with me,' and then Maiden stuck her. I mean the damn knife went all the way in, right in her gut. She tried to scream, but she couldn't, and Maiden took that knife out and stuck her again, like four or five times."

She was still lying there, blood everywhere, when Maiden bent down and spit on her.

"'That's for being such a great mommy,' she said. I'd taken my mask off, too, and I still remember Connie looking up at me, like 'you, too?'

"I wanted to run, but Maiden told me to follow her, and I did.

"Beverley was in the bedroom, passed out lying lengthwise across the bed. I remember Maiden said, 'This is too easy.' And then she took that butcher knife and grabbed him by the hair so his head was high enough that she could reach under. She slapped his face a couple of times, and he came to. He was looking into her face when she slit his throat.

"'Thanks for all the good times, Daddy,' is what she said while he just gurgled and bled to death there on the bed. She said she wanted to make sure he knew what was happening and who did it."

Then she handed the knife to Buddy.

"She told me I was in on this, too, and I should get at least one good lick in. I took the knife, which was all sticky with blood, and I stabbed him. Overkill, so to speak."

They went back to the foyer, where Connie Broom had finally bled out.

"You know what Maiden said? She said she was hungry. So she went over to the refrigerator where there was some Smithfield ham. She took it out and made us a couple of sandwiches. We just sat there, with Connie twenty feet away and Beverley back in the bedroom, both dead, and we had dinner."

Their plan was to go back to the friend's house and then come back the next morning and discover to their horror that they were orphans.

"But Maiden was covered with blood by this point, and she said she figured that it wasn't going to be all that easy to get away with it. I've got to say, she maybe wasn't thinking that clearly anymore.

"What she proposed was Plan B: We would pack a few things, take the car, and go to Virginia Beach. She had the combination to the safe in the bedroom, and she took a couple of thousand dollars, which seemed like plenty.

"She said we'd let them find us down there. We'd tell them that we decided to take the car and just go to the beach for a couple of days. We could say we decided that after we left Susan's house the next morning."

Buddy says it didn't sound like that great an idea to him, but that he was more or less in shock.

"I mean, they needed killing," he says, "but still, it kind of shook me."

I allow that patricide will do that to you.

"Not Maiden," he says. "She didn't flinch a goddamn bit."

They took turns driving to the beach. On the way, Maiden had Buddy stop the car long enough for her to pitch the murder weapon into a ravine a mile from their home. Then they stopped at a rest stop on the Interstate, changed clothes in the car, then went inside, and cleaned up as best they could.

They found a motel that would take cash from a kid who obviously was not twenty-one. Maiden got the room so no one would see them together.

I call the chief to tell him I'm OK and discourage any rash actions on the part of his troops.

When I hang up, I ask Buddy again when I'm going to see Maiden.

"All in good time," he says. "When I'm through telling you my story."

He says they hung out for a couple of days, going to the beach and eating junk food.

"But then we turned on the TV, and there we were."

The friend back in Staunton had broken and told the cops what she'd promised not to tell. It was all over the news. The phrase "manhunt" was used often.

"Maiden cussed and threw a lamp against the wall, and then she got real quiet. After a minute or two, she said she had a plan. I told her that her plans up to this point hadn't worked so well. She told me this one would."

What his sister proposed was that they split up.

"She said they would be bound to find her soon, because of the car, but they didn't have to catch both of us."

She made him gather up the scant belongings he'd brought with him and she had him take a taxi to the bus station. She gave him an address in Richmond. There was a guy there, she said, who was good at producing fake IDs. She knew because he'd done it for her and her friends so they could get into clubs. She said he might be able to slip away, start a new life "because the old one is damn sure over."

"She said that, if they caught her, she'd swear that she hadn't seen me since we left her friend's house Halloween night, that I was going to meet some girl but she didn't know who.

"She said she was going to go away, too, as soon as she had a chance to pack. She told me to meet her at the train station on Staples Mill Road two days later at eight in the morning. We'd take a train somewhere and start over."

Buddy says he saw later how hopeless that was, but at the time there didn't seem to be any other option.

"If we'd have been able to stick with the plan," he says, "it might have worked, except Maiden's friend would still have ratted us out.

"She gave me a hug at the bus station, told me I was the only real friend she had in the world and that we'd be together again.

"Of course, we weren't, not for a long time."

She also gave him most of the money she'd taken from their father's safe.

He figures the cops must have found the car, and Maiden, not more than a couple of hours after he left.

"She never gave me up," he says. "She might have gotten a lesser sentence if she had, but she stuck with her story that she had no idea where I'd gone. Of course, she also stuck with her story that strangers killed our parents, that she was on the way to the beach when it happened."

While Maiden Broom was being caught, tried, convicted, and sentenced to life in prison, Buddy was reinventing himself. He says he dyed his hair brown, bought a pair of glasses in a drugstore, purchased a turtleneck to hide the scar on his neck, and connected with the fake-ID purveyor.

"So I became James Caldwell. The guy didn't ask any questions, and after a couple of days holing up in a cheap motel on the Jeff Davis Highway, I hit the road again."

He went to Chicago, and then to Minnesota, then out West, taking jobs that paid cash and didn't check backgrounds.

"Eventually I created this whole new me," he says. "I was pretty good with my hands, and there were always contractors looking for cheap labor. I was basically in the same boat with the Mexicans and Guatemalans, working for cash and laying low."

He says he knocked around the country for three years before he wound up in LA, where a guy with a fake Social Security card told him where he could buy one.

"Just like that," he says. "Two hundred bucks for a whole new me as James Caldwell."

He says he knew somebody must be looking for him.

"I mean, Maiden said she did it herself, but they had to wonder about my just disappearing the same night both our parents were murdered. Still, with her convicted, maybe finding me wasn't a top priority, you know?"

He knew his sister was in prison in Virginia, and he says he used a computer in a public library to find out exactly where.

With the Social Security card, making a new identity wasn't that hard. He says he was able to enlist in the army.

"Did eight years, including two tours in Iraq. When I got out, it wasn't hard to find good jobs. And that old scar, well it was from an IED blast over there. Nobody questioned that."

He eventually wound up back in Richmond and runs, or maybe "did run," a company that renovates old houses and flips them.

"That's how I got to know Dogtown," he says.

He says that for years he was afraid to write to Maiden, for fear it would tip off anyone still looking for him. Finally, though, he got the nerve to contact her, as James Caldwell, "an old friend." He got a post office box in Richmond and used it for a return address.

"Finally, about ten years ago, I worked up the nerve to visit her there. We hadn't seen each other in fourteen years, but it was like I'd only got on that bus yesterday."

He says she told him, when they could talk with a small amount of privacy, that she would be free someday, and that she had some scores to settle. She asked him to help her settle them.

"I told her I was there for her, no matter what," he says. "There wasn't anything I wouldn't have done for her. I mean, she took the rap for me."

I don't mention that maybe without Maiden, he wouldn't have had to spend the rest of his life on the run, that the worst problem he would have had would have been working through a fucked-up childhood, and who hasn't had one of those?

"Honestly I figured it was an empty promise," he says. "And then, right after Christmas, I got that call."

Somehow the parole board had seen fit to release Maiden Broom, figuring that thirty-three years was punishment enough for killing both her parents. She had told him it might be possible, but he didn't believe her until it happened.

"She finished high school and got a college degree while she was in," Buddy says. "She said she had been a model prisoner. But she told me, when we were riding to Richmond after she was released, that they, quote, bought her act. I knew then that Maiden was like a damn elephant: She never forgot."

He says he wasn't thrilled when he came to realize that she meant to enlist his help in righting perceived wrongs.

"But she was my sister, all the family I have, and I owed her."

And so Buddy Broom, relatively successful business-man, was drafted to find a place where his sister could hide out until she got her pound of flesh. He knew about the house we're in because he'd tried to buy it himself. He had had a key made, and the two of them moved in one night.

"She said I didn't have to be part of it, but that she needed a place to stay out of sight, and she needed a car. And a big-ass knife."

So he bought her a secondhand Toyota, $500 down.

"She bought the knife herself."

He says she actually had a list of who had done her wrong.

"I tried to talk her out of it, but then she fixed me with one of those stares that used to scare the shit out of me when we were kids and had a disagreement. Bottom line, I did what she told me to do."

He knew, as soon as the paper ran the story on Harlan Bell's murder, that the rampage had started. He'd seen the list.

"When she came back with that finger, it really freaked me out. She said it was just a souvenir, a way to keep score."

He says she would return after every "adventure," slip-ping into the squatter house after driving up the alleyway, usually at night with the lights off.

"She even took the car out to pick up food," he says, "but you know that, since you wrote about it. She's been more careful since then."

I ask for confirmation that she was indeed the one who butchered five people over the past three weeks.

He shakes his head.

"Six," he says. "Have somebody check with the Staunton paper and see if a Mrs. Susan Fincastle wasn't murdered in a home-invasion incident last week. Little road trip."

"The friend who didn't cover for her?"

He nods his head.

We've been in here for forty minutes and four calls to L.D. when I ask him again, more insistently this time, when the hell Maiden is going to make an appearance.

He shakes his head.

"Won't be any appearance."

Not being a complete idiot, this does not completely surprise me, but his smile chills my ass.

"See," he says, "Maiden ain't here. Maiden's gone hunting."

CHAPTER TWENTY

YESTERDAY AFTERNOON, Maiden went for a long walk. Buddy says she wore a wig and sunglasses, so she felt fairly safe.

On the way back, she saw what I did: a cluster of cars that looked suspiciously like police issue. So she backtracked.

"I was in here," Buddy says. "She called me and said it looked like the jig was up. She said she was sorry she'd caused me so much trouble."

He laughs.

"She saw you too."

Buddy could have either taken the car or he could have holed up and hoped that somehow the cops would go away. He chose Plan B, which didn't work so well.

"We had a strategy, in case either or both of us got caught here," he says.

"So where did Maiden go?" I ask. "Where is she?"

"That's what I really wanted you to know," he says. "See, Maiden had one more big grudge out there, against the snooping son of a bitch who busted her."

I'm starting to get a very bad feeling.

I'd like to strangle the bastard, but he does have a gun.

"Where," I ask, as calmly as I can manage, "is she?"

He gives me an address in the Fan with which I am well familiar.

"She wanted to make sure you were here when I called her on her cell. She wants to talk to you."

Despite the cold, I can feel sweat gathering under my armpits.

"If she's done anything to my family . . ." I begin.

"What?" my interviewee says. "What are you going to do? Hell, she knows her goose is cooked, and mine too. You're a smart guy. You've got to know that, with what I've told you, I'm probably never going to see daylight again."

His grin is as cold as this room.

I reach for my cell phone, to call the chief.

Buddy grabs my wrist and takes the phone from me. He throws it against the wall, where it shatters.

He turns back to me.

"So should I make the call?"

I swallow and nod.

A few seconds later, he hands me his phone, and I hear the voice of the entity, the ghost I've been chasing the last couple of weeks.

"Well, well," she says. She has a voice that reeks of old-money Virginia, still there after all those years locked away in prison. "It's so good to hear your voice at last, Willie. You've been up in my business quite a bit lately, haven't you?"

"Where's my daughter?" I ask. "Is she there?"

"Oh, she's fine for now. But I'm afraid she's not going to be fine for much longer."

"Are you there?"

"Absolutely. And your grandson is adorable, by the way. It's a shame really."

She explains that she took a bus and then walked the rest of the way.

"Please don't hurt her," I'm in begging mode now. "Take me. It's me you want. I'll come over and you can have your revenge on me."

I hear her laugh.

"Oh, no. That'd be too tricky, Willie. No, I think I'll just leave my little plan like it is. I'd rather think of you living with it. All that guilt. A whole family wiped out. If you'd just left me alone."

I need to let L.D. know where she is. I remember that Andi was going to be home this morning and was going to go with William over to my mother's after she got him up and dressed.

I ask her about Walter, my son-in-law.

"Oh," she says, "he's gone."

My sphincter clinches.

"What do you mean, gone?"

She says she doesn't mean gone like to his reward, "not yet." She saw him from across the street leaving the house.

"Your daughter says he went out to get some eggs. Being your daughter, Willie, I'm sure she wouldn't lie. What a surprise for him when he gets back home."

I tell her she'll never get away with it.

"Fuck," she says. "I know that. My life ended back in 1988, when they sent me away. Do you think it was wrong, Willie, to murder my parents after my father used me for his fuck toy and my mother just let it happen? But everybody ganged up on me. It was just me and Buddy against the world. Still is."

She says she'd planned for years what she would do if she ever got the chance. She's made a list of all the people who were responsible for her spending her adult life in a prison cell "just in case somebody was ever crazy enough to let me out."

She says she thought using the same kind of knife she'd used on her parents decades ago was a nice touch.

"And Buddy was there for me, just like he said he'd be. My one true friend."

She says something else too.

"Buddy won't tell you what they did to him, but he and I both know we had more than enough reasons to make ourselves instant orphans.

"We thought we might actually be able to get away with it, maybe go to Canada or something, new identities, maybe pass ourselves off as husband and wife. Wouldn't be the kinkiest thing the Broom family ever did.

"But then you had to stick your big nose in, so I just had to add one more name to the list.

"So now we're just going to make a little statement, Buddy and I are. We're going out with a bang instead of a whimper."

I ask her if Buddy is on board with all that. He's close enough to me that he can hear her. I see her brother nod his head even before she affirms it.

I try to keep her talking, hoping to buy some time, but she hangs up.

When I call the number back, I get voice mail.

I'm ready to make a run for it, gun or no gun, when I realize that Buddy's not behind me anymore.

I hear a door open. And then I smell the gas, much stronger this time.

When I look around, Buddy's gone into the front part of the house. He's standing there, on the other side of the opening, and the smell is suddenly overpowering.

He's standing in the middle of the next room. He has a book of matches in his hand.

"I'm going to give you a break," he says as he looks over at me. "Although by the time Maiden gets through with your daughter and maybe your grandson, it might not be a break after all."

With that, he reaches into the box and pulls out one match.

"Better hurry," he says.

I am almost to daylight when I hear him strike the match. I'm just outside, running like I haven't run in thirty years, when the blast knocks me off my feet.

CHAPTER TWENTY-ONE

I OPEN my eyes. I seem to still be among the living, unless L.D. Jones has joined me in the afterlife, God forbid.

He's leaning close and talking. I can see his lips moving. But I can't hear him. Despite the January cold, my back-side feels warm.

Then, for some reason, a couple of cops are dragging me away.

Eventually I can hear a little out of my right ear, ironi-cally the one that got mutilated a couple of years ago by a demented individual with family issues who missed my brainpan and only slightly marred my good looks.

When I try to communicate my concerns to the chief, he doesn't seem able or willing to understand me at first. I realize later that he was distracted by the structure behind me being sent into orbit by Buddy Broom's match and some natural gas.

Finally he understands. I repeat the address for Andi and Walter's Fan house so that I'm sure he has it.

"Hurry," I croak. Then I must have blacked out.

✦ ✦ ✦

WHEN I come to, a couple of paramedics are bending over me. They seem to think I need medical attention.

Fuck that. I'm on my feet and, after grabbing one of their shoulders to steady myself, head for my car.

Gillespie and others come over to hinder me. I tell them all to get the hell out of my way, and then I'm in the Honda.

Gillespie is pounding on the window. He looks like he might be about to light up my ass, but something stops him. As I start the car and drive away, I look in the rearview mirror and see him shrug and shake his head. Chauncey Gillespie's nobody's idea of the model cop, but to my knowledge, he's never shot anybody in the back, especially if they haven't committed a crime.

The trip to the Floyd Avenue residence of my daughter and her family takes either an eternity or fifteen minutes, according to whether we're talking about perception or real time. I do recall running a couple of red lights, but since a goodly portion of the city police force is over dealing with the aftereffects of a structure blowing up in Dogtown, nobody with a badge bothers to take offense.

Floyd is a wide street, by Fan standards. However, by the time I'm a block away, I see that it has become reduced to one lane. Cop cars and paramedics, a kaleidoscope of red and blue lights, block my way. I pull in behind the last emergency vehicle and tumble out, then take off running toward Andi and Walter's townhouse.

I am tackled by a couple of Richmond's finest a few houses down. I might have shoved one of them. At any rate, they are in the process of arresting me, probably after giving me a good tasing, when I get it through their thick skulls that my daughter and her family are inside the house that is the object of their clusterfuck.

"Ah, hell," one of them says. "It's that goddamn Willie Black."

They let me go forward, but there's a phalanx of police just outside the front door. L.D. Jones stands in their midst and comes down the steps, meeting me on the sidewalk.

"Easy, Willie," he says. "Easy. It's all under control. You don't want to go in there now."

"The hell I don't."

Just then, the door opens, and four EMTs come out carrying a gurney with a white sheet over what obviously is a body beneath it. My legs nearly buckle.

Before anyone can stop me, I run up to the gurney. Before they can pull me away, I yank the sheet back.

And there she is.

It's the first time I've seen Maiden Broom. In death, she looks her age. The wig she was wearing is slightly askew, and the hair beneath is more gray than blonde. Her mouth is twisted in what, were she alive, might be interpreted as a sneer. Her eyes are open.

The sheet, pulled farther back, reveals great patches of reddish-brown at three spots in her chest and abdomen.

And, around her neck, where Maiden Broom in another life might have been wearing a string of pearls, is the necklace. Those ten fingers, some more withered than others, sewn onto the twine.

The chief pulls me back.

"Crime scene, Willie," he says, and I finally relent.

He sees the question in my eyes.

"No more victims," he says. "Just the one. It was all over before we even got here."

He finally lets me up the steps.

Inside, in the living room, Andi and Walter sit with William between them.

The adults seem to be in shock. Young William appears to be more entertained than traumatized.

"Daddy shot the bad lady," he explains.

✦ ✦ ✦

THE STORY comes to me in drips and drabs as first Andi and then Walter, with six-year-old William assisting, tell it.

Andi was in the breakfast nook when the front doorbell rang. My grandson was watching cartoons on the TV in the den. Walter had just run out to buy some eggs at the market down the street as Maiden had said.

"She just pushed her way in when I answered the door, and she had this big damn knife . . ."

"Big damn knife," William concurs.

"You never should open that door unless you look first," Walter says, and Andi says she did, but she figured it was just some neighbor.

"She looked harmless."

Apparently Maiden wanted to terrorize my pregnant daughter and my grandson for a bit before killing them. Andi said she made her go into the den, where William was, and then she made them sit down beside each other.

"She was talking crazy," Andi says. "She said you were out to get her, and that now I'd find out she was not a person to be taken lightly.

"She said she warned you."

I can only nod.

"I tried to talk to her, but she just kept talking over me, like I wasn't even there."

Andi shivers.

"I was going to charge her. She was going to have to kill me if she tried to hurt William.

"But then Walter came back."

I have never thought of my son-in-law as a macho man. I mean, he's an accountant, a skinny guy who wears glasses and a pocket protector. He considers one beer to be a night on the town. We get along, because he takes better care of my daughter than I ever did, but he's not the kind of guy who likes a dirty joke or to close down the bar.

He does, however, pack heat. I never knew that until today.

He keeps a pistol locked and loaded in the trunk of his car, a fucking Glock 19. When he saw the front door ajar, he went straight to the car, then slipped inside the house while Maiden was delivering her monologue and scaring my daughter shitless.

Walter says he got to the door leading into the den before Maiden knew he was there.

"She turned around when she heard me, and then she started coming toward me with that knife."

Walter immediately appreciated his advantage, having brought a gun to a knife fight.

"I shot her," he says, simply. "Four times, I think."

He says his father taught him how to handle a gun when he was a boy. That's one lesson Peggy, my only parent, never got around to teaching me.

There's blood all over the floor. Andi has some spattered on her blouse.

"We've got to clean up this mess," she says and starts to get off the couch. Walter catches her arm.

"We're going to get you a clean blouse," he says, "and then we're going out somewhere, get us a nice brunch. By the time we get back, the police will have sorted everything out."

William gets up too. He comes up to me.

"Grandpa," he says, "I wasn't scared."

I try to throw my arms around all three of them at the same time.

As I'm leaving, I go up to my son-in-law.

I say the only words I can think to say.

"Good man."

CHAPTER TWENTY-TWO

Sunday, January 24

Because of COVID concerns, we can only seat six at our back table at Joe's, with no one allowed on the outside, because it's too close to the booth across the aisle.

Cindy and I are joined by R.P. McGonnigal, Andy Peroni, Custalow, and his on-again, off-again main squeeze, the lovely and talented Stella Stellar.

Andy and R.P. want to know all the details. Abe has already brought Stella up to speed.

"He shot her ass?" Andy says. "Damn, I didn't think he had it in him."

I answer in the affirmative.

"Man," Stella says, running a hand through her hair, which is purple today, "you're just a shitstorm magnet, aren't you, Willie?"

It's worse than that, I tell her. A magnet just sits there and waits for things to attach themselves to it. I seem to have a knack for actively wooing disaster.

"Yeah," Cindy says. "You're such a lightning rod that anybody close to you is liable to get struck."

She sees that maybe she's hit a nerve.

"Sorry," she says. "I know you didn't mean to get Andi or William involved."

Cindy has a point though. We all knew Maiden Broom had my whole family on her radar. I should've done more to protect them.

"The worst part of it," my beloved says, "is that he wasn't even on the payroll yesterday. Well, he wasn't until about three o'clock anyhow."

✦ ✦ ✦

THREE O'CLOCK is about when I made a rare trip to our publisher's office.

Sarah sent Leighton Byrd to Floyd Avenue, along with Chip Grooms from photo, when she got word that the prime suspect in the Dogtown Slasher killings had been gunned down. By the time Leighton and Grooms got there, though, I had the situation well in hand. After all, I had an interview with the shooter and the kidnap victims, who also happened to be family, in addition to my exclusive with newly departed Buddy Broom.

"Are you sure you're not too close to the story to write it?" Leighton asked. "Or a little concussed?"

I could tell she desperately wanted me to let her put her byline on what's probably going to be the story of the year in Richmond, but I assured her that I was perfectly capable of filing a story about the attempted massacre of my family.

I wasn't sure of that, but no way in hell was I going to let little Leighton have this one. In addition to the killer's demise, I had the tape recording of Buddy Broom's tale of woe and insanity.

"You've got plenty on your plate already," I told her, "what with the parole board and the mayor and all."

Yes, our star junior reporter has had a busy enough past two weeks without needing to horn in on my territory.

She wound up writing two stories for Sunday's editions anyhow.

One of them was about how the chief of the parole board has taken a leave of absence. I don't think he said anything about spending more time with his family, but they're going to be seeing a lot more of him whether they like it or not. Releasing a handful of people who were never supposed to see daylight again, without even notifying their victims or victims' survivors, has inflamed the populace. Even the governor has the dogs nipping at his heels. He doesn't get to run for reelection, but he still doesn't want to be remembered as the guy who let our parole board turn people like Maiden Broom loose on the citizenry. Hell, he might want to run for the Senate someday.

Speaking of politicians, Leighton's other story for our dwindling readership is about our mayor's future plans. It seems that Hizzoner has decided not to seek the Democratic nomination for lieutenant governor after all.

He made the announcement yesterday, not long after my son-in-law plugged Maiden Broom.

"I realize that my passion and abilities will be better used as mayor of our great city," he said. "Those urging me to run for higher office tried to get me to stay the course, stay in the race, but my calling is here, as your mayor."

Actually, Leighton told me, she had it from a trusted source that the money guys who were going to back the mayor had urged him to exit off that course as soon as possible. Ever since it became known that he kept the wrong man in jail for days while all logic indicated that the Slasher was still out there, his higher aspirations had fallen into the realm of wishful thinking.

"I hope Chief Jones doesn't do anything wrong for the next three years," Leighton said. "I have it on good authority that the mayor would like to send *him* to spend more time with his family."

I told Leighton that I wouldn't worry too much about L.D., who always seems to know where the bodies are buried.

So after making a run by Perly's for a pastrami and Swiss on rye to go, I wandered into the newsroom.

There were only eight people in the place, about average for a Saturday afternoon these days.

They all came over in a touching display of newsroom camaraderie.

"Are you OK?" Sarah asked.

"Don't I look OK?"

"Well, um, not so much."

I told her that sleeping in a Honda, being the only witness to a killer's final statement, having a house more or less blow up on me, and then having most of my family nearly wiped out by a maniac probably had taken its toll. Plus, I told her, I could probably use a shave.

"And a change of clothes," Sarah suggested.

I told her I'd be writing two stories, one on the Slasher's death and one on the last words and testament of her hapless brother.

"First, though, I've got to have a few words with the publisher."

I knew he was there, because I saw his fucking Rolls in the parking deck.

Sarah, reading the malice in my eyes, urged me to be careful.

I reminded her that she was talking to someone who'd almost died and nearly lost his daughter and grandson chasing a story he wasn't even getting paid to chase.

"If he wants the goddamn story," I told her, "he's going to have to come up with some of that quid pro quo."

She reminded me that, right or wrong, he was the publisher.

I told her I'd keep that in mind.

I realized I was starved. After people stopped asking me questions, I ate about half the sandwich.

Then I went to the breakroom for some newsroom coffee. I didn't pay, and it was worth every penny.

And then I went upstairs to see Benson Stine.

Sandy McCool, the suits' longtime and long-suffering administrative assistant, wasn't there to guard the gates, so I managed to let myself into Stine's office unannounced. He appeared to be the only one of our brain trust who was in on a Saturday afternoon. I'm always amazed at how many of these vice presidents and other idiots are still drawing paychecks while the newsroom starves.

"Willie," he said, frowning but not telling me to get the fuck out either. "What are you doing here?"

He hadn't been out of his office and doesn't know what's been going on in his city. I brought him up to speed.

"Well, that's wonderful," BS said as he stood. "What a story. Both stories. Have we put it on the website yet?"

I explained that we hadn't put it anywhere yet, and that we wouldn't unless he did something for me.

Stine sat down and frowned a little deeper. He is not used to the peons issuing ultimatums.

"Since last week," I told him, "I have been furloughed, which means I am not getting paid."

He started to sing the tired-ass song about the necessities of furloughs, doing more with less, orders from corporate, blah-blah-blah.

I interrupted him.

"I don't really give a damn about any of that," I told him. "I've been out there, on my own time, damn near getting myself killed, almost getting two of the people who matter most to me killed, just to get this story.

"Well, I've got it now. Got two of them, as a matter of fact. And if you want them, you're going to do something for me."

He told me I was pressing my luck. I told him he was pressing his.

He looked like he wanted to throw me out, but Benson Stine is a smart man. He figured that, even though he was twenty years younger, he might not be successful, might instead get his ass kicked. At that point, I welcomed the opportunity.

So he listened for a change.

"If you want those stories," I told him, "I'm not on furlough. I haven't been on furlough and will get back pay for every fucking day I've flogged this story for free. I figure I've given you about twelve hours a day since the fifteenth, but I'm a generous guy. I'll only charge you for eight."

He made all kinds of noise about the company not asking me to work. I told him that was true, but if I had been working on my own time the last eight days, then he'd have to pay me like a freelancer, and that my freelance fee was coincidentally the same amount I'd have earned had I been on the payroll.

"The clock is ticking," I told him. "Those two stories aren't going to write themselves."

In the end, he buckled. He called the chief money guy and, somehow, they worked it out.

"See," I said when he told me I'd be getting paid, "wasn't that easy?"

He glared at me.

"Your days around here might be numbered," he said.

I told him that, if history was any teacher, I'd be around here longer than he would. I've seen some publishers come and go.

He didn't say anything to my back as I walked out.

I wrote the lede, managing not to insert myself into that one, other than to note my relationship with Andi, Walter, and William McGinnis. By the time I'd backfilled all the mayhem Maiden Broom had effected this month, the damn thing ran more than eighty inches.

Being old school as well as old, I cringe at a story that long, but nobody gives a shit these days. Content is a welcome stranger. Hell, last Sunday we had exactly five staff-produced byline stories in the A section. Everything else was wire copy or stuff other state papers ran a day or two earlier. The rest of the section was erectile dysfunction ads and entreaties to invest your life savings in fake coins.

The other story, the one in which Buddy Broom aka James Caldwell gave what amounted to a dying man's confession, did require some liberal use of the first-person pronoun. Thank God for the tape recorder, because the explosion that sent Buddy to his reward or punishment left me a little loopy. That one was another eighty inches.

By the time I'd packed it in, about eight cups of coffee later, I was ready for a nap. Sarah edited it herself, so I felt reasonably sure it'd be clean.

Neither of us left the building until after eleven. Sarah asked me if I wanted her to drive me home, since my general condition did not seem to have improved in the last few hours.

I told her about *my tête-a-tête* with BS.

"And he's going to do it?"

I nodded.

"Damn," she said, "maybe I ought to go demand a raise."

I advised her not to press her luck.

"You're too young for Social Security, and we don't have a pension plan anymore."

✦ ✦ ✦

At Joe's we toast ourselves this chilly Sunday morning with cheap Bloody Marys and manage to run up a bill approaching a hundred bucks after hogging Joe's best table for two hours.

Our server mentions that one of the other joints in what we jokingly call the Brunch District has a nice big table in the back that could accommodate a dozen of us.

When R.P. tells her that we like it just fine here, she mutters something that sounds like "too bad" as she walks away.

Goat Johnson calls from Ohio, and we put him on the speakerphone. He says he's in quarantine because the guy who was doing a makeover of their kitchen tested positive. He knows about as much about the Dogtown Slasher as our local readers, having bought an online subscription.

"So she cut off their damn fingers?" he asks.

After she killed them, I tell him.

"Ah, that's OK, then. I thought she was some kind of weird sadist or something."

I tell him that the families of Harlan Bell, Jack and Sheila McCaskill, Lemuel Cartwright, and Kizzie Long might say she was sadistic enough. Plus my daughter and her husband. Plus the late Susan Fincastle. We still haven't gotten to the bottom of that one yet, but unless Buddy Broom was lying, she's Maiden's sixth victim. The cops are investigating.

Andy adds that his tomcatting friend is lucky he wasn't the seventh.

"That'll teach him to keep it in his pants," Cindy tells her brother.

"He's a slow learner," Andy replies.

Cindy and I drop by Laurel Street on the way home. We know that my daughter, Walter, and William are there.

"I can't believe they even let you have life insurance," Peggy says by way of greeting her darling boy.

I tell her that it wouldn't surprise me if the Grimm Group were to drop me. I tell her how I came to get my salary reinstated.

"Good boy," my mom says. "Don't take any shit."

That's always been high on Peggy's list of parental advice. She used to say it to me as I left for school in the morning in lieu of "have a great day" or "study hard." As the single parent of a mixed-race kid in the whitest and roughest neighborhood in Richmond, she was prone to be an advocate of tough love. Now, though she's seventy-eight and I'm sixty, her mantra has not changed.

Cindy notes that if I were to take a little shit once in a while, I might not be in constant danger of cashing in on that life-insurance policy.

"Well," Peggy says as young William comes up to her and begs her to read him a story, "I guess she's right. I don't want him to get his ass killed."

William looks up at me, solemn as a judge.

"Don't get your ass killed, Grandpa," he implores.

I tell him that I will try very hard not to.

✦ ✦ ✦

CINDY AND I are back at the Prestwould shortly after one. Clara Westbrook has just made it up the front steps after enjoying her own brunch at the Country Club of Virginia after a spiritually uplifting morning of Episcopalian grace.

"Willie," she says, "you surely do know how to find a story, don't you?"

I tell her that sometimes they find me.

Clara's eighty-four now, one of my favorite people in our twelve-story insane asylum. Her lungs and her heart are going to fail her someday soon, I'm afraid, and we'll be a poorer place without her.

"Have you heard about Mr. Feldman?" she asks.

"Did he pass?" I ask hopefully.

"No. And don't talk like that, Willie. It's bad luck to wish people dead."

Clara's one of the few people here who puts a "Mr." in front of Feldman's name. Mostly we just use his sobriquet, McGrumpy, or just refer to him as "that asshole."

It turns out that Feldman, who's almost as old as Clara, has started wearing a mask inside the building and has gotten his first COVID shot.

What, I ask, brought this on? A rare burst of sanity? Concern for his fellow man?

"Oh, nothing like that," Clara says.

Feldman, it seems, is in love.

It turns out that a woman about half his age has started coming around to "visit."

Clara can get anybody to let down their guard, even McGrumpy. He told her that his new sweetie, who probably weighed Feldman's age, general appearance, and cussedness against his bank account, had apparently come out in favor of the latter.

"He told me she said there'd be no more . . ." here, Clara has to stop to giggle and catch her breath. "He said she told him there would be no more 'good loving' until he started wearing a mask and got vaccinated."

It will take me some time to scrape the vision of McGrumpy and "good loving" from my brain.

"So," Clara says as we go our separate ways, "are you going to stop trying to get yourself killed and act like an adult?"

I tell her that if I wished to act like an adult, I certainly wouldn't be working as a newspaper reporter.

CHAPTER TWENTY-THREE

Tuesday, January 26

Maiden broom won't go away.

She's been dead three days now, already cremated by the state. Her closest living relative, her uncle back in the valley, had no desire to deal with her in death as in life. Carson Broom said yesterday, right after he threatened to sue my pants off, that cremation was an appropriate end.

"She's going to be burning a lot longer than that," he said.

Maybe so, but she's risen from the ashes, so to speak.

As for brother Buddy, they cremated what they could find of him. That gas explosion pretty much scattered his ashes already.

Three Richmonders seem to have profited from this unholy mess. Between the murders and the fuckups by the parole board and the mayor, Leighton Byrd and I got enough material out of this to win ourselves a cheap press award or two. Leighton is already updating her résumé.

Cindy suggested that I polish mine.

"You know, in case somebody finally does kill you, I can use it for your paid obituary."

At the newspaper, when I trotted out the old saw about reporters going in after the battle and shooting the wounded, Leighton shrugged and said, "Well, somebody's got to do it."

It does appear that Buddy was right about one thing. The unlucky Susan Fincastle, who betrayed her old friend Maiden Broom so long ago, probably was Victim No. 6. They're checking DNA, but fingerprints seem to bear that out.

And, of course, Marcus Green always comes out smelling like a rose.

His lawsuit against the city on behalf of the late Sylvester "Sly" Simms looks sure to yield a settlement large enough to assuage the grief of Sly's long-lost brother, who didn't seem to know or care where he was or how he was until he was falsely targeted as the Dogtown Slasher and then hanged himself.

When I suggested again that Marcus donate his one-third of that settlement to perhaps a homeless shelter, he chuckled and again promised to get back to me.

So Maiden is gone, but she is not forgotten, and most certainly by her uncle.

He was on my to-call list, but he beat me to it.

His call yesterday, the one threatening litigation, came while I was sipping coffee and trying to ignore the entreaties of Butterball and Rags, who thought food might be in the offing.

"You know that's all bullshit, right?" he said.

It took a while to find out who was calling and what manure he was referencing.

He had read the tree-killers I wrote for the Sunday paper and the follow-up yesterday morning, and he had issues.

One in particular.

"There wasn't no damn stuff going on between her and my brother," he said. "That's just something her and Buddy cooked up."

I asked him how he knew that, and he told me.

Carson and his brother were close.

"Beverley told me everything, the good and the bad, and there was plenty of bad."

A few months before he was murdered, Beverley Broom spilled it.

He had suspected for some time that his son and daughter were a little too close.

"Hell, they slept in adjoining bedrooms, and there wasn't any damn lock on the door, I can tell you that. They weren't natural. That's why my brother and that crazy wife of his kept sending her away to boarding schools, to keep them apart."

It didn't work, Carson said.

Beverley told his brother that Maiden was going to have to have an abortion. He knew a doctor at the big teaching hospital in Charlottesville who would do it on the QT.

"Did he know who the father was?" I asked.

"She told him! She didn't even try to hide it. Said she and Buddy were in love, and that there wasn't anything he could do about it."

The plan was to send Buddy to some prep school as far away from Staunton as could be arranged, as soon as Maiden was back from "the procedure."

I am a cynic by nature and by trade.

"That's an amazing story," I told Carson Broom, "but can you prove it? I mean, what if your brother was just covering up for his own sins?"

"If I couldn't prove it, goddammit, I wouldn't have called you. My brother's good name has been besmirched, and I'm the only one left to defend it."

Carson said he found the proof after he moved into his late brother's house.

"I was cleaning stuff out. It took me a damn year to get rid of all the crap they'd collected."

He finally got around to what had been Maiden's room.

"And I found the pictures. I almost missed them. She had put them between the pages of a book, and when I picked up the book, they fell out. I took pictures of them on my iPhone camera yesterday, and the kid who does the yard work showed me how to send them, so I'm going to email them to you, if you'll give me your address. And then I want a damn correction."

I gave him the email address. Five minutes later, they showed up.

One of the photos was obviously of a teenage Maiden and Buddy, taken with a timer, I guess. They were both naked, sitting side by side on a bed. The other one was of Maiden sitting naked atop Buddy, who seemed to be enjoying the experience. She has her head turned toward the camera, her middle finger extended.

When I called back, I told Carson that his evidence was pretty compelling.

"But what if she was doing the nasty with the father too?"

He had a pretty good answer for that one.

"Beverley was impotent. Nobody much but me and, of course, his wife, knew it, but he hadn't been able to get it up for years. Probably alcohol-induced."

I could hear Carson clear his throat.

"Look, my brother wasn't a saint. He and Connie were hard on those kids, sometimes maybe too hard, but he did not have sex with his own daughter, and I want you to straighten that shit out, or I'll sic the lawyers on your sorry ass."

I asked him if he ever offered up any of this salacious information in court.

"They never called me to testify," he said, "and I wouldn't have told that crap anyhow. My family is fucked up enough without me adding to it. She was going to prison, and that was good enough for me, although I did wish they had caught Buddy too."

I promised Mr. Broom that I would look into it and get back to him very soon. He assured me that everything he said on the phone is for public consumption.

✦ ✦ ✦

EVERYBODY'S DEAD except Carson Broom, so I guess he gets the last word. When I went into the office a few hours early and told the story to Sarah and Wheelie, Wheelie's first concern was that we were going to get sued. I'm not even sure that Carson, as the dead man's brother, has any standing, although I'm certain Marcus Green could bring me up to speed.

But I'm a big fan of the truth, and I convinced my editors that the version I wrote for the Sunday paper, Buddy Broom's version, was not the whole story or even the real story. I showed them the photographs on my iPhone. We all agreed that the paper couldn't run those.

"They're underage," Sarah said, as if that was the only prohibition. "You probably ought to delete them."

But we can describe the incriminating shots, I explained, and we do have a live witness who can tell what he knows.

They finally agreed that I could write the story, Carson Broom's version. It won't accomplish much except to maybe rub some dirt off a dead man's reputation.

It ran this morning. Carson Broom called to thank me and said he probably wasn't going to sue after all.

Maybe I'm getting too old for this shit. Buddy Broom had convinced me with his story when it is obvious he was just stalling so his sister/lover could have time to ruin my life.

Over breakfast, I tell Cindy that maybe my bullshit detector has died of old age.

She says that anyone who can sling it as well as me should still be pretty good at sniffing it out.

Before reporting to work, I need to go by Laurel Street.

I need to say thank you.

Peggy might never have been nominated for mother of the year, but it occurs to me that the days of my misspent childhood on Oregon Hill could have been a lot worse.

HOWARD OWEN

This is **Howard Owen's** 21st novel and the 12th in the Willie Black mystery series. Owen, a longtime newspaperman, has worked at everything from reporter to sports editor to editorial pages editor. He has been writing fiction since 1989. He and his wife, Karen, live in Richmond. Among his earlier novels are the best-selling *Littlejohn* and the Willie Black mystery, *Oregon Hill*, which won the Dashiell Hammett prize for best crime literature in the United States and Canada.

Lightning Source UK Ltd.
Milton Keynes UK
UKHW011953030123
414791UK00004B/70